BOOK ONE

MINDSPACE

INFILTRATION

A K DUBOFF

www.cadicle.com

Published by Dawnrunner Press
Cover Copyright © 2021 A.K. DuBoff

ISBN-10: 1954344112
ISBN-13: 978-1954344112
Copyright Registration Number: TX0008730706

0 9 8 7 6 5 4 3

Produced in the United States of America

TABLE OF CONTENTS

CHAPTER 1

CAPTAIN KIRA ELSAR raced through the desolate concrete corridor past darkened research labs. "Retreat!" she shouted into her comm.

Behind her, footsteps echoed from deeper within the underground MTech facility. Too many footsteps.

A shout sounded behind her, then a spray of plasma fire lit up the hall. Kira's HUD politely informed her that hostile forces had been detected nearby. *Really helpful, thanks.*

She ducked behind a collection of pipes protruding from the wall. It was terrible cover, but she'd take what she could get.

Glancing toward the exit, she noticed Ari peeking around a bend in the corridor.

"I thought I ordered a retreat, soldier," Kira said over her comm.

"That was before you got yourself cornered," Ari Lanmore, a lance corporal on her team, replied. "No one gets left behind."

Kira couldn't help grinning behind the blacked-out faceplate of her helmet. She loved Tararian Guard honor, especially in a time like this. "Lay down some cover fire on my mark. I'm going to try some fancy footwork."

"You've got it."

"Now!" Steeling her resolve, Kira bolted from behind the pipes.

Her powered armor propelled her down the hall while plasma blasts flew in either direction. She'd only gone three strides when a new warning flashed on her HUD—the concentrated enemy fire was about to overload her suit's defenses. Without thinking, she spun in a series of swift circles to diffuse the load on the armor's electrified skin.

After seven awkward strides of spinning and skipping, Kira made it to the corner where Ari was hunkered down. She leaped the final step to safety.

"Ma'am, you are a graceful angel," Ari said over the comm. His opaque helmet hid his face, but there was no mistaking the amusement in his voice.

"We speak of this to no one." Kira snatched a concussion grenade from a pouch on her tactical belt and tossed it back down the hall, then she pressed herself against the wall.

Ari followed her lead.

A moment later, Kira's HUD lit up with a flash and heat signature. The helmet muffled the explosion, but she could feel it reverberate through the wall at her back. *Try walking away from that, fokers! That's what you get for burning my new armor.*

Dust and debris flew down the corridor. When the particulates began to settle, Ari poked his head around the corner.

"Clear," he announced. "You do realize that your entire dance down the hall is documented on my combat recorder, right?"

"And that will be filed with the mission report and shown to no one." Kira glared up at the huge soldier through her faceless helmet.

"Yes, ma'am, I'd never think of sharing."

Liar. The video would be uploaded to the galactic Net before dinner. She'd be a viral sensation.

Kira rolled her hazel eyes. "At least select a tasteful song to set it to, okay?"

Ari bust out laughing again. "I was thinking it'd go great with—"

The walls shook anew with a concussive boom and series of thuds.

What in the stars was that? Kira swapped places with Ari and refreshed the info display on her HUD. When she checked the hall around the corner, she was greeted by the sight of a mech twice her height.

A volley of kinetic rounds flew from the gun mounted on the mech's right shoulder.

"Hello to you, too." Kira took off full-speed down the side hall with Ari close behind.

"I thought this place was supposed to be abandoned!" Ari shouted.

"Yeah, well, our intel was wrong." Kira reached an intersection and turned to the right, in the direction her HUD indicated was the exit. "Asher, Boro," she raised the two other members of her team on the comm. "We're coming out hot."

"Looks like you're having quite the party, ma'am," Nia Boro replied. "I have a direct link into the local Net. I think I can lower a blast door and seal off that section."

"Do it, for foksake!" Kira reached another intersection, this time turning left. "ETA on—"

"Done! You're almost to threshold…"

Kira spotted the thick, metal strip in the ceiling and along the walls. As soon as she and Ari passed through, the blast door began to lower.

The mech charged for the door. Kinetic rounds pelted the blast shield, a handful making it under the metal slab. Kira and Ari flattened themselves along the side walls of the corridor to avoid the enemy fire until the shield was secured.

Kira let out a long, deep breath. Though thuds continued to sound against the blast door, there was no way the mech could get through the meter-thick barrier. "That could have gone better."

"We do have some good news," Kyle Asher offered over the comm. "When you had to abort the data retrieval at the alpha location, we headed to the beta target. Location is secure. Plan B is still an option."

"Good." Kira assessed the relative position on her HUD. Provided there weren't any more unexpected mechs, it should be a straight shot through another wing of research labs. "We're on our way."

Kira's team was an unusual structure within the Guard— her as a captain in command of three lance corporals—but their unique specializations related to information extraction had kept them together as a unit longer than most. Situations like this when they came under unexpected enemy fire were rare, but she wouldn't want anyone else to have her back.

Ari took point as they jogged down a side hall toward Nia and Kyle's location. The corridor was lined with doors, and a handful of the labs had observation windows. The rooms inside looked to be sterile chambers, some of which had exam tables in the center surrounded by an array of equipment. At least no one seemed to be around in *this* section of the supposedly abandoned facility.

"Creepy much?" Ari commented.

Something about the stark white environment and empty medical rooms did make Kira's skin crawl. "Yeah," she replied, eyeing every surface for potential threats.

As if on cue, an overhead light began to flicker.

I'm really starting to hate this place. Kira suppressed her nerves and stayed focused on the mission at hand. "I hope the data archive has answers and I didn't scuff up my new armor for nothing." She frowned at the newest pit on the left arm of her sleek, black armor, which had been sustained during the latest volley of kinetic rounds.

"Better dents in the armor than holes in you."

She couldn't argue with that.

The corridor terminated in a set of windowless double-doors. Ari cautiously cracked open the right door and peered into the hallway beyond.

"Shite… you've gotta see this." He stepped into the room and held the door open for Kira.

Her breath caught as she took in a bank of holding cells. Clear plexiglass covered the fronts of the tiny rooms, each containing a cot, toilet, and sink. The rooms looked like they'd been used.

"So much for this being a typical MTech research lab." Kira walked over to the nearest cell and examined its interior. Her HUD picked up gashes in the white plastic of the side wall. "Are those claw marks?"

"The configuration is more like a person's hand." Ari's tone was dark.

"Normal nails couldn't do that. Not even close."

"Could this be connected to the Bakzen's genetic experimentations during the war?"

Kira shook her head. "The Bakzen didn't have claws—they

were more or less like us. No, this is something different."

"Regardless, why the fok would a civilian research lab have holding cells like this?"

"For nothing good." Kira took a calming breath. "Come on, we need to get to the others. There's no knowing if any more of MTech's guards will show up and try to kill us."

Without another word Ari resumed jogging down the hall, keeping watch to either side in case someone—or something—was in one of the cells. He'd been assigned to the team of technical specialists as their muscle, and his commitment to that role had gotten the team safely out of worse situations than this.

Kira followed him at a slight distance, mentally running through the possibilities. *Those stupid fokers in intel. They throw out shite and we have to clean up the mess.*

The assignment was supposed to be simple: scope out an abandoned Mysaran research facility on the remote moon and scour the data archive for any reference to the Elusian government. Like many of the border worlds operating independently from the Taran Empire, not everyone wanted to play nice all the time. The Mysarans had been particularly obstate of late and were looking for any opportunity to pick a fight with their Elusian neighbors.

As the public-facing branch of the Empire's military might, the Tararian Guard had been called upon to run interference and keep the situation from escalating. Of course, it wasn't the Guard's place to police non-Empire worlds, but Kira's team specialized in gathering information that no one knew was being gathered. At least, that's how it was supposed to work; throwing grenades tended to undermine the stealth part of a covert ops mission.

The Guard clearly hadn't been given the whole story.

Whatever was going on, Kira would get to the bottom of it—even if her armor did have to get some scrapes along the way.

After eighty meters, the corridor of cells opened into a square room filled with what appeared to be monitoring and surveillance equipment. An archway at the back led to another passageway. According to Kira's HUD, the two other members of her team were in an adjacent room. She swept her gaze around while she walked toward the door, recording it for later review. Maybe they could get more clues if the data archive didn't have the complete story.

She exited with Ari and traversed the short distance to the room where Nia and Kyle were waiting. The door was ajar.

Instead of just Kyle and Nia, though, there was a middle-aged man tied to a chair. He was wearing a white jumpsuit and looked pissed.

Kira stopped in the doorway. "You didn't tell me you had a guest."

Nia's helmet was off, exposing her slicked-back black hair. She shrugged, a smirk highlighting her dark features. "Well, I said we had secured the beta location. We just need a little help with the rest."

"I thought you'd hacked into MTech's local Net?" Kira asked.

"We did," Kyle confirmed, shaking his head of close-cropped brown hair, "but the data we're after is locked up behind some kind of firewall with encryption I've never seen before. We can crack it, of course, but how much time do you want to spend on this? A password would be much faster."

Minutes made all the difference when there were enemies breathing down their necks. It was obvious why the man was strapped to the chair.

Her team was looking at her. They knew what she could

do—it was why she was the leader of a team of soldiers a head taller than her. For all Kira's comparative physical limitations, she could do what no one on her team—or anyone else in the Guard—could: read their captive's mind and extract the information they needed.

Kira swallowed. "I don't have the authorization."

Nia glanced at the man tied to the chair. "Then, ma'am, it is unlikely we will be able to access the encrypted files and fulfill the mission objective before enemy forces reach our position."

Protocol existed for a reason. Telepathy and mind-control were a slippery slope, and specific rules were the only way to keep things civilized. But, the mission was at stake.

Easier to ask for forgiveness than permission. Kira nodded to her team. "All right. We need to know what's going on. Someone wasn't honest about why we were sent here."

Relief filled the faces of her teammates.

The man in the chair shrank back. "Wait, what are you going to do?" he asked, a quaver in his voice.

Kira popped the latch on her helmet and slid it over her head. She massaged the fingers of her gloved hand over her scalp to fluff the pixie cut of her red hair. "You're going to tell me the password to access that encrypted information one way or another."

The man shook his head. "I don't know it."

It didn't take a telepath to know he was lying.

"Are you sure you want to do this the hard way?" Kira questioned.

He didn't reply.

"All right." Kira took a step forward and focused her hazel eyes on him. He tried to look away, but Kyle placed his hands on either side of the man's head to make him face forward.

"What is your name?" Kira asked the man in his mind.

"Stewart," came the response.

Good, he hadn't been trained in any mental blocking techniques, like the ever-present guards Kira maintained around her own thoughts. This would be easy. Kira dove into his mind using the methods she'd been training in since she was a child.

Her homeworld of Valta was known for the unique properties of the natural ecosystem, where animals across the world shared telepathic bonds. When people had settled on the world and consumed the native resources, they found that certain members of the population developed telepathic abilities of their own.

Valta's colonists and ecosystem had been studied for generations. Despite the research efforts, it was still impossible to predict who'd develop abilities—there was no apparent genetic link, and no one born offworld had ever developed the unique form of telepathy, even when fed a diet of plants and animals from Valta. Given that unpredictability, it was considered an honor to have telepathic gifts emerge, especially since no one was sure exactly how the abilities worked.

Valta's telepathy was a distinct skillset from the telepathic and telekinetic abilities expressed by the Gifted in the rest of the Taran population. Those individuals often trained as Agents in the Tararian Selective Service—or TSS, the military complement to the Guard known for its unique telekinesis training program. However, that had never been an option for Kira. The telepaths among her Valtan people were an anomaly, neither normal nor Gifted under conventional definitions. While powerful enough to both read minds and compel others, her Valtan telepathy required direct eye contact to initiate a connection, and she had none of the other advanced physical manipulation skills which fell under the 'telekinetic' nomenclature of the Gifted.

So, Kira had jumped at the opportunity to join the Guard at eighteen, promised she'd be able to use her abilities for a greater purpose than entertaining tourists on her homeworld. Most of the time, she believed that she was able to make a difference for the better. But times like this, when she had to violate someone's mind against their will, turned her stomach.

It's for the mission, she reminded herself, deftly navigating the layers of Stewart's mind to seek out the information residing just below the surface of his consciousness. The funny thing was, the more someone wanted to hide something, the easier it was to locate.

Kira found the compartmentalized part of Stewart's mind related to his work. *"What is the password?"* she asked in a soothing mental tone.

He struggled against her, vain attempts at resistance in her mental vise. After a moment, he gave in. The alphanumeric string filled her mind, and she memorized it.

"Thank you," she told him, then retreated.

As soon as she broke eye contact with Stewart, he sucked in a sharp breath. "How did you do that?"

"Wouldn't we all like to know," Kira replied, then stepped over to the computer terminal. She entered the password she'd extracted from Stewart's mind.

The display screen flashed acceptance of the access code.

Nia grinned at Kyle and Ari. "She's good."

"Just doing what's necessary for our mission," Kira said under her breath. "Where's that external drive?"

"I'm on it." Kyle plugged in a portable drive to copy the encrypted files off the local network.

He'd modified the device from the base model, making it one of the most efficient and secure data extraction tools available. Complemented by Nia's brilliance with both hardware systems and coding, the duo were regarded as the preeminent hackers in the Guard. When combined with Kira's telepathy and Ari's expertise in weaponry, the team hadn't yet met an obstacle they couldn't overcome.

"What do we do with him?" Ari asked with a nod toward Stewart.

"Leave him," Kira instructed. "We need to get out of here ASAP."

"Transfer is at ninety-two percent," Kyle reported.

Kira nodded. "Gear up. We're busting out of here as soon as it's done." She slipped her helmet back on and verified that no new enemies had yet registered on the sensors feeding into her HUD.

"Done." Kyle extracted the drive and handed it to Kira.

She placed it in a secure compartment in the breastplate of her armor. "Good job, all. Let's get out of here."

Ari, Nia, and Kyle headed out the door.

"You shouldn't dig into this," the prisoner cautioned before Kira left the room.

"Why?" she asked.

The man shook his head. "Unless you want to be in the middle of a war, you should leave well enough alone."

"Are the Mysarans planning a move against the Elusians?"

Stewart barked a laugh. "You think this is just about the Mysarans?"

"Well, this facility is owned by MTech, and they're based on Mysar, so—" Kira began.

"Right, yeah. Have fun with those files." Stewart chuckled.

"No, tell me." Kira took a step toward him, ready to take off her helmet.

"We have company!" Ari shouted over the comm.

Kira assessed the enemy situation on her HUD—it was only five security guards, but they were between her team and the exit. Answers would have to wait.

She detached her plasma rifle from the holster integrated into the back of her armor. *Looks like we're shooting our way out.*

CHAPTER 2

"REMIND ME TO yell at the boss for sending us in here without backup." Kira shot at one of the security guards barring her path.

"No one was supposed to be here," Nia said while squeezing off two quick shots at another opponent.

They were trying to incapacitate rather than kill, but the enemy was being a pain in the ass about it. After a few more carefully placed shots, Kira's team was able to force the enemy into a side hall so they could go around them to access the exit.

It was time to run for their lives.

A plasma beam streaked past, two centimeters from Ari's head. "Play nice!" he spun around and landed a precision shot in the offending pursuer's leg.

Kira brushed her left hand over the drive tucked away in her armor. *Whatever we have here, MTech doesn't want us to leave with it.*

Too bad.

They reached the secondary entrance that they'd flagged as

an emergency egress point while planning the op. Fortunately, the facility didn't seem to be fully staffed with security or they would have been trapped.

Kira ushered her team through the outer door. Ari hung back to lay down a barrage of suppressive fire to buy seconds for the run to their landing shuttle on the surface of the barely habitable moon.

The team piled into the shuttle through the back hatch, and Kira took the controls. "Come on, Ari!" she urged.

Gunshots sounded from the direction of the facility exit.

"On my way."

Kira powered up the shuttle, waiting for her final team member to run on board.

"I'm in. Go!" Ari hit the controls to close the back hatch.

Even before the shuttle's door had sealed, Kira lifted the craft from the ground. The craft launched on a steep, upward trajectory at a dizzying speed. They slipped off their helmets once the interior had pressurized.

"That was close." Kyle released a slow breath.

Nia slumped back in her seat as the artificial gravity kicked in. "Didn't they run any thermal scans of the facility before we went in? It should have been obvious it wasn't abandoned."

"Yeah, someone certainly knew it wasn't," Kira replied. "Whatever information we have, someone wants it very badly."

"Don't accidentally drop the drive and smash it to bits," Ari jested.

"No worries. It's right up against my boobs—I protect that region at any cost." She patted her chest.

Ari cast her a sidelong glance.

Kira narrowed her eyes with playful challenge. "Yes, soldier, that's closer than you'll ever get to them."

He shrugged. "I will continue my admiration from a

respectful distance in the shower."

Nia smacked him upside the head.

"What? Yours are nice, too," Ari added.

Nia exchanged an exasperated eye-roll with Kira and left it at that. It's not like the ladies hadn't done their own comparisons of their male counterparts—they were just more discreet with their conversations.

Kira activated the auto-pilot. "When we get to the *Raven*, how about—"

A violent jolt rocked the shuttle.

"The fok?" Nia checked the scan. "Shite, they just fired a missile at us!"

"Where'd that come from?" Kira instinctively activated the stealth mode and then took over manual control to alter course, hopefully enough to throw off any other weapons locks. When she'd completed the evasive maneuver, she consulted the scan data on the holodisplay. Sure enough, a hidden defensive launch array on the surface was aimed at them.

"They're nuts to shoot at a Guard ship!" Kyle exclaimed.

Ari frowned. "Or desperate."

Their shuttle wasn't large, but it was packed with the Guard's best tech. Even with a direct hit, it was unlikely anything the weapons array could send in their direction would do any significant damage—and with the stealth systems activated, the ship would be invisible. But, that was beside the point.

"How in the stars did MTech get these kind of armaments?" Kira murmured.

"This might explain it." Kyle added a holographic overlay over the front viewport.

Their interstellar Guard ship, the *Raven*, was in orbit at the spinward horizon line from their present position, but there was also a new ship, which hadn't been there at the time they headed down to the moon for the op. ID tags marked it as Mysaran military.

"Shuttle 1, proceed to berth immediately," a familiar voice broke in over their shuttle's comm.

"Major Sandren, what—" Kira started to ask.

"You were never on the surface of that moon and this Mysaran cruiser never saw us," her commander replied.

Checking the scan again, Kira realized that the *Raven*'s stealth was also active.

"Yes, sir," she acknowledged. "On our way." She ended the comm link.

Nia's brow pinched with concern. "What kind of shitestorm did we just stumble into?"

Kira shook her head. "I don't know, but I want answers."

Operating on auto-pilot for the rest of the short voyage, the shuttle looped a quarter of the way around the moon before meeting up with the *Raven*. At two hundred meters long, it was just large enough for a small crew to not go crazy if they were cooped up for more than a week or two. A cargo hold underneath the matte black vessel provided berthing for two pods.

The shuttle directed itself into an open bay door protected by a force field. As soon as the shuttle was on the deck in its usual slot, the outer hatch slid closed over the hold's opening.

Kira rose from her seat at the controls. "I'll hand over the loot and see what Sandren knows."

Ari's eyes gleamed, his spirits already recovered from their recent firefight. "While you do that, I have to, uh, file my report with the combat data."

Kira sighed; true to form, Ari could shrug off any amount of combat if he had a new video project to obsess over. "Shite, that's right…"

"What now?" Nia asked.

"You'll see soon enough," Kira grumbled, shooing her team from the shuttle.

She parted ways from them when they headed for the showers so she could debrief with their commanding officer. She'd been under Major Lucas Sandren's command for the past two years, and he was her favorite CO to date in her nine years with the Guard. Though he'd been rough on her at times, he was fair and had never sent her into a mission without a thorough, accurate briefing. Until today.

Sandren was in his office behind his compact desk. He leaned forward in his chair. "Captain, I—"

Kira slammed her hand on the interior control panel to close the door. "With all respect, sir, what the fok?"

"I didn't know. I wouldn't have sent you in there alone if my intel had been accurate." Sandren looked genuinely contrite.

Kira's shoulders slumped. "We weren't properly equipped for a firefight like that. We almost…"

"But you made it out."

"And then they kept shooting at us! What's a Mysaran cruiser—"

"That was an unexpected wrinkle, yes." Sandren fixed his brown eyes on her. "Were you successful?"

"Yeah, barely." She retrieved the portable drive from the pocket on her chest and tapped it against the open palm of her left hand. "What is this?"

"The higher-ups have been tight-lipped about the whole thing. You did your part."

Something about his tone indicated he might know more than he was letting on, but Kira was too tired to argue. "The

MTech guy I spoke to said this wasn't just about a potential civil war with Mysar. Whatever it is, there's some foked up shite going on down there."

"The presence of the Mysaran military made that much clear." Sandren took the drive from her and stared at it in his hands. "Right before you docked, word came down that they've increased the security clearance on the op."

"Retroactively? That—"

"I know." Sandren nodded solemnly. "We'll debrief back at base."

— — —

Monica Waylon braced for the worst. "How much did they get?"

"Enough," her assistant, Tim, replied. "Phase One and Two trial reports, expression models, the analysis of—"

Monica held up her hand to stop him; ultimately, the details didn't matter. Her research with MTech had been exposed. The bomaxed Taran authorities were threatening to ruin everything, as usual. Years of effort would be for naught if she couldn't keep the project moving forward.

"At least the test subjects had already been relocated," Tim offered.

It was small consolation, but Monica needed to embrace any good news at her disposal. "Yes, there is that."

Even though she was the project's director, she still had superiors watching her every move. They'd been berating her for months about the expense of her new research lab on Valta, but she now felt vindicated—having anticipated that they'd need a facility with better security. Her proactive preparations meant that their work in the new Valtan lab could continue without drawing additional unwanted attention, whereas the raid would have spelled disaster if they had still been operating solely out of the moon lab. However, if the Tararian Guard was intent to intervene, she'd be forced to take drastic action.

Monica smoothed her shoulder-length brown hair. "I'll update our benefactors about our status. Check on the Phase Two subjects."

Tim eagerly rose from his workstation. "Right away."

She watched him go. He'd been spending too much time with the subjects recently—getting attached. Their work demanded complete loyalty to the cause, and they couldn't afford such distractions. She made a mental note to look into how Tim had been spending his visits to the holding cells; he was just as disposable as the Phase One subjects.

For now, though, her collaborators were awaiting her call.

As soon as Tim had entered the cellblock, Monica logged into the secure platform she used to communicate with her associates. Her digital avatar—a gray, androgynous figure—appeared in the holoconference on her behalf. She was soon joined by the representations of two of her associates, Nox and Reya—blue and green figures, respectively.

"The situation isn't good, but it's salvageable," Monica stated.

"What was the Tararian Guard doing at the moon?" Reya demanded.

"The better question is, why was that lab still inhabited?" Nox countered. "We were assured that it would be empty."

"There were delays in transferring the rest of the weapons cache," admitted Monica. "Unfortunately, that retrieval team hadn't wiped the local servers yet. If I'd had warning, I would have tried to make other arrangements."

Reya's green avatar shook its head. "Two hours later and

the Guard wouldn't have found anything meaningful."

"These are the risks of operating in the shadows," Nox said. "Once the Empire's prying eyes are no longer on the Elvar Trinary, we can operate freely."

Monica's eyes narrowed. "But the Empire *is* involved now. And they're persistent."

"We do have contingency plans in place," Reya offered. "Is it time?"

Nox's blue avatar nodded thoughtfully. "Yes, I may have a solution that will solve all of our problems."

— — —

President Elton Joris of the Elusian Alliance was certain his Mysaran neighbors were up to something devious. He was no stranger to their political posturing, but unusual fleet activity coupled with rumors about MTech's research over the past several months had put him on high alert. At least his contacts would soon be able to tell him just how much danger Elusia was really in.

Maybe we should have invested more in our military, but how were we to know Mysar would move against us? He prayed that it wouldn't come to that. The Elvar Trinary had been settled by their ancestors to *escape* war; he hated to think a civil dispute might rip them apart.

A knock sounded on his door.

"Enter," Joris stated.

Nico cracked opened the door and slipped inside. "Sir, I verified that the new draft of the reunification agreement includes those language modifications you requested."

"Good. Thank you for coordinating that review," Joris acknowledged. Nico was young, but he'd proven to be a capable and dedicated assistant. Given what Elusia might be facing in the near-term, he'd need members of his administration he could trust.

"Sir, I was wondering…" Nico began tentatively.

Joris waved him the rest of the way into the office.

Nico closed the door and approached Joris' desk. "Sir, about those changes regarding the defense assurances… Are you concerned about Mysar?"

Capable, dedicated, and *astute*. Joris folded his hands on his desktop. "I began these discussions with the Taran Empire because it is my belief that we should mend ties with our Taran brethren. I hope Mysar sees fit to follow our lead."

"And if they don't?"

"Then we won't be alone."

CHAPTER 3

HOT WATER WASHED over Kira's body, releasing the tension in her muscles from the last several hours. She could use more than that, but it would have to wait until she was back in her private cabin at the Tararian Guard outpost she called home; no need to add any more ammunition to Ari's arsenal.

She turned off the shower and stepped out, wrapping a towel around herself. The shared bathroom was large enough for six people at once, but she had the place to herself at the moment.

I wonder if we'll get any answers back at the station? Given the major's reticence, she doubted it. But she could hope.

With MTech headquartered on a planet in the same system as her homeworld, she was more familiar with them than some of her reconnaissance targets. She'd never had any reason to think of them as anything other than a respectable biotech research company, but any private corporation with military ties always put her on edge. If MTech was indeed working on a secret project with the Mysaran military, she didn't like the potential implications for her loved ones on Valta.

Kira dressed in a clean shipsuit, her standard garb while on any spaceship or station. The interior elastic material fit snugly against her body like a second skin, providing protection in the event of a rapid decompression. A black outer layer offered pockets and weapon holsters for practical use, and quick-release pouches in the collar and around the cuffs contained an emergency helmet and gloves to complete the pressure suit. Given the amount of tech packed into the garment, it was surprisingly sleek and flattering—though the tight fit always did take several minutes to get used to each time she put it on.

Her team was waiting for her in their shared quarters down the hall. The four of them had slept, eaten, and trained together nearly every day for the past four years, and it had made them as tightknit a group as any in the Guard. Though she was officially in command, any time they weren't on an active op, she would rather just be one of the team. They were friends, and that friendship kept them safe when it mattered most.

"Learn anything?" Kyle asked as soon as Kira stepped through the door. He was perched on his bunk above Ari's against the right wall of the compact room.

"Squat." Kira closed the door and leaned back against it.

Nia, on the upper bunk to the left, tilted her head, her dark eyes narrowed. "We can't do our job effectively if they keep secrets from us."

"Don't I know it." Kira shook her head.

"We can't let it happen again," Ari grumbled.

"What am I supposed to do? Sandren was fed bad intel—he didn't know, either. We have to go in and do what we're told. We've trained to be prepared for anything, and we showed that today."

The large soldier crossed his arms, highlighting the

substantial muscles under his tight shipsuit. "I still don't like it."

"Well that's the nature of the job. Quit moaning," Kira shot back. She pushed off the door and took the two steps to her bunk. "We got the job done today. That's what counts." She collapsed on the mattress.

"The Guard has more than enough means to have anticipated we'd run into problems," Kyle insisted.

Kira flourished a hand. "Yes, someone lied. We can speculate all night about what MTech was up to, but we won't know for sure until someone tells us."

"One of those times I wish I'd been able to download the info to internal storage so I could look at it myself." Kyle's youth on Lynaeda had given him a leg up when it came to technology, being one of the so-called 'tech head' planets in the habited band of Taran worlds situated between the core worlds and outer colonies. He was surprisingly un-modded for someone of his background—no AI pairing or significant body augmentations—but that was probably what had attracted him to the Guard's sensibilities in the first place.

Admittedly, Kira shared his regret that they didn't have a copy of MTech's data for their own review. "Best not to get ourselves worked up about it," she said.

Kyle sighed. "Yeah, I know."

"They *did* shoot at us. I think we have the right to be a little cranky," Nia pointed out.

Ari straightened on his bed across the narrow gap from Kira. "Speaking of cranky, your newest video will be paired with 'She Can Move'."

Kira rolled her eyes. "That song is terrible."

"I knew you'd love it! It's oh so appropriate."

Ari was lucky he was half a meter taller than Kira or he'd

have a boot in his face. He was the brawn of the group—a weapons specialist paired with two hackers and a telepath—but he had a good head on his shoulders and a big heart, in addition to being one of the best marksmen in the Guard. As much as Kira razzed him for his video-posting obsession, it amused her to watch the huge man take such care and attention to sync up the music with visuals. So long as that attention to detail continued to carry over to his planning of the team's loadout for ops, she didn't have complaints.

All the same, Kira couldn't let him get away with the videos forever. She had been quietly plotting her retribution—a practical joke that would leave Ari begging for mercy. He'd never see it coming.

"Since the dire matter of musical accompaniment has finally been resolved and we're at a dead end with the MTech investigation, who's up for a game of Fastara?" Nia asked.

"Sure, why not?" Kira agreed, eager for a distraction. She had been about to suggest the same activity for the jump home before they'd been so rudely shot at by the MTech missile-launcher.

Kyle hopped down from his bunk. "Come on, Ari. The video editing can wait."

The other man groaned. "None of you are any fun."

Kira rolled her eyes. "Oh, I know, it's *shocking* that I'm not thrilled about your entertainment coming at my expense."

"Hey, I'm turning you into a celebrity. You should be *thanking* me." Ari grinned.

She gave him a dagger-glare as she rose from her bunk, knowing it would carry more weight than any punch she could land on him—and was more professional.

Ari swallowed. "Um, yeah, a game of Fastara sounds great!" He followed the rest of the team out of their cabin.

Their go-to gaming spot was the galley, not far down the corridor from their cabin. Though there was a proper rec space on the deck below, having proximity to snacks always made the game more enjoyable. There'd been a few mishaps along the way in that respect early on, but a mandatory napkin rule had eliminated card grease and salt smudges.

Kira grabbed the galley's designated Fastara deck from a storage cabinet near the pantry and got situated in her usual seat at the table. She soaked in the ethereal blue-green light of subspace shining through the viewport—still an incredible sight after nearly a decade of traveling between star systems.

"Who's dealing?" Kira asked her team.

"I will," Kyle volunteered, sitting across from her. "I won't have any more of Nia's nonsense like the game on the way out here."

Nia smiled innocently. "The universe saw it fit for me to deal myself winning hands."

Fastara had been spacefarers' staple entertainment for as far back as anyone could remember. Even growing up on a backwater planet, Kira had spent many nights in her youth playing the game. The complex rules took time to pick up, since there were a lot of contingencies based on the specific cards in play. Her team had set their own house rules, as was customary—incorporating favorite practices from each of their backgrounds. Nia had often found ways to exploit her own house rule, which favored the dealer, but it was all in good fun.

Kyle began dealing out the plastic playing cards, with the colored symbols face-side down. "First person to ten?" he asked.

"Of course," Kira confirmed; they never played any other way, but they always asked just the same. She evaluated her hand once Kyle finished dealing—a pair and several run potentials depending on what was dealt into the common pool.

"Blue dominant," Kyle stated, as was his place as dealer to set the high suit for the round.

Nia groaned when she saw her own cards. "My lucky streak has ended."

"Thank the stars for that." Ari, to Kyle's right, laid down a blue pair as his opening move.

Kira could work with that.

They went around the circle several times, playing cards when they could and drawing when they were unable to make a move. After the common pool of cards built up a little, Nia got the telltale glimmer in her eyes that she was sitting on something good in her hand.

"I'll trade you for the green diamond," Kira offered, trying to anticipate her friend's move.

"Not a chance," Nia declined.

Bomax, she's going to block me. Kira knew she had already lost the round, though it wouldn't be realized for a few more rotations. The competitive side of her was miffed, but she'd learned long ago that it was important to keep the game in perspective. It was sport among friends, nothing more.

"Aaand, bam!" Nia laid down a perfectly structured run in her hand, connecting to two common pools on the board.

"Shite!" Ari threw down his cards.

"I'm sorry, I can't help being so awesome." Nia beamed, clearly pleased with herself for turning around a terrible hand.

Her sharp wit and adaptability made Nia an asset to Kira's team. Unlike Kyle being born practically with a computer in his hand, Nia had led a simple childhood on a freighter. She was entirely self-taught, learning computer systems by effecting repairs on her parents' aging ship. The youngest on the team, she still had some growing up to do, but Kira was certain that Nia had a bright future in the Guard—provided she didn't kick the wrong general's ass in a game of Fastara.

"Successful round?" Major Sandren ask, coming down the corridor from the access ladder.

"Yes, sir!" Nia gloated.

"Depends on who you ask," Kyle grumbled.

Sandren chuckled. "Good to see you're recovered from the firefight earlier." He headed for the refrigerator.

Kira smiled. "Sweet victory is the best way to get over a sideways op, sir."

"Not that you'd know anything about winning." Nia playfully elbowed Kira.

"Hey, I came in second. Cumulative points, my dear. I'm still in it."

Nia eyed her challengingly. "Uh huh."

Sandren selected a bottle of juice from the refrigerator and then walked over to the table. "You all performed admirably under the circumstances today. Command asked me to pass on their thanks."

A thank you? The op follow-up kept getting weirder and weirder.

"Did they find what they were looking for in the info?" Kira asked.

"We'll know soon." Sandren nodded to the team. "Enjoy your game." He departed.

Once Sandren entered his cabin, Ari leaned forward over the table. "All of this feels… off."

"For sure," Kira agreed, "but nothing we can do about it now."

Nia gathered up the cards to shuffle the deck. "You heard the major—we're under orders to enjoy our game."

"Your turn to deal," Kira said. *We may as well play while*

we can. She had a feeling that things were about to get serious.

— — —

Colonel Terence Kaen reviewed the information extracted from the MTech lab. It confirmed his worst fears.

Shite! Those sick bastards don't know when to stop. As he flipped through the pages of lab reports on his tablet, his face paled the more he saw. They were going to lose containment on the situation if they didn't act fast.

MTech, the preeminent research institution in the sector, was based on the planet of Mysar. The Mysaran Coalition was the most aggressive of the three planets in the Elvar Trinary near the border of current Taran Empire territory. Colonists had set out to the fertile system several hundred years before, settling Mysar, Elusia, and Valta in an attempt to escape the chaos in the Taran Empire surrounding the war with the Bakzen. While Elusians valued peace and harmony as they established their new culture on the border world, Mysarans had followed in the grand Taran tradition of conquering and expanding. Caught in the middle was Valta, a lush garden-planet with such unique properties that it was at constant risk for exploitation.

As a policy, the Taran Empire didn't get involved in civil disputes. However, Elusians had expressed a desire to rejoin the Empire now that the Bakzen conflict had been resolved and the corrupt Priesthood on Tararia had been overthrown in the post-war aftermath, so the ongoing tension with Mysar was a concern. Kaen himself had gone to meet with the leadership of the Mysaran Coalition three years prior, and they insisted there was no cause for worry. All the same, the Tararian Guard was poised to step in covertly if the situation continued to escalate—and it was undoubtedly trending in that direction.

Kaen dialed President Elton Joris of the Elusian Alliance. Few individuals had a direct line to someone in such a position, but Kaen's task demanded the utmost discretion, and that meant no intermediaries.

The president answered after ten seconds, his piercing blue eyes and white hair contrasting against the dark background of the room. "Colonel, do you have news?"

"The team was able to retrieve the data archive, sir. It's not good."

President Joris groaned. "What did you find?"

"They've completed their first live trials."

"This is a nightmare." He wiped his hands over his face. "Is the Guard prepared to take action?"

"We're standing by to assist, sir, but we're in a tough spot so long as Elusia isn't officially in the Empire."

"I know, I'm working on it." The president paused. "They've built a new lab on Valta. We need to get someone on the inside to find out what they're doing in there."

Kaen nodded. "I know just the person."

CHAPTER 4

THE FOLLOWING MORNING, the *Raven* arrived at Orion Station, the Tararian Guard outpost where Kira was presently attached. SiNavTech's network of navigation beacons made interstellar subspace travel easy and quick, especially with the Guard's long-range jump drives.

"Are your mission reports filed?" she asked her team as they debarked from the *Raven.*

"Yes, ma'am," Ari replied. "There has been a *full* report of the mission."

Kyle and Nia snickered.

That bomaxed video... Kira rolled her eyes. "I have to go meet with the brass."

Nia's eyes sparked. "I wonder if Kaen has seen the video of your dancing?"

"Hey, that mission is classified," Kira reminded them. "If command catches wind that you leaked classified documentation, don't expect me to save your necks."

Momentary panic flashed across Ari's face, then he

relaxed. "You almost had me for a second."

Stars, she really did care about her team too much, and they knew it.

"Just… don't push your luck. I'll see you later." She jogged away for her scheduled meeting with Colonel Kaen.

Under normal circumstances, Kira would have cursed the stars for needing to endure an audience with one of the most notoriously rigid, domineering officers in the Guard. This time, though, she wanted answers. If getting that information meant turning the charm up to eleven with the hardass officer, she'd do it.

The administrative section of the Guard base was situated at the center of the star-shaped space station, where it would be the most protected in the unlikely event of an enemy assault. Each arm of the star configuration contained a central concourse leading to starship berths and bays for the significant complement of fighter craft.

To expedite her trip to the center of the facility, Kira hopped in a car along the maglev track running the length of the concourse. At the central hub, she exited the car and jogged the rest of the way.

After pausing to make sure her shipsuit was in regulation compliance, she knocked on Kaen's office door.

"Enter," a baritone voice called from within.

Kira plastered on her most professional smile and entered. "Hello, sir. You wanted to see me?"

"Have a seat, Captain." Kaen gestured toward a metal chair across from his desk.

"Thank you, sir." She sat down but didn't bother to get comfortable. Prior experience with that particular seat had revealed it was impossible.

"I understand that you ran into some trouble at the MTech

lab."

He has such a way with understatement. Kira nodded. "Yes, sir. Our intel said the facility was abandoned, but we encountered armed guards and a military assault mech."

"A mech? Indoors?"

"Barely fit in the hallway, sir."

Kaen frowned. "I'm glad your team was able to fulfill the mission objective despite those setbacks."

'Setbacks'? That's how he's going to play it? Kira leaned forward in her chair. "Sir, may I speak freely?"

He gave the hint of an exasperated sigh but quickly composed himself. "Permission granted."

"Someone doctored the mission brief."

Kaen studied her. "What makes you say that?"

"The resistance we encountered wasn't some new arrival that walked in moments before us. They had been there, and there wasn't any shielding around the facility to have hidden the thermal outputs. Someone knew that facility was occupied, but the Guard wouldn't have received data retrieval authorization for an active private lab. They wanted us to think it was abandoned so we'd go in." Kira crossed her arms.

"I can't deny the possibility," Kaen said after a ten-second pause.

"Was it you, sir?"

The colonel's eyes widened. "Why would I put one of my best teams at risk like that?"

"Because you knew we could handle it, like we did."

"Your team is quite skilled." Kaen folded his hands on the desktop. "Few others would have been able to access those files."

That was a roundabout admission of guilt, if ever there was one. But why? "Before we left, the man I... 'interrogated'...

indicated that there's something going on with the Mysarans, and potentially beyond that."

The colonel gave a slow nod. "The Guard's responsibility is to assess threats and carry out orders in the best interest of the Taran Empire. You have performed admirably in retrieving information to support those goals."

If a career in the Guard hadn't worked out, Kaen would have made a bomaxed good politician. Kira flashed a prim smile. "Happy to do my part, sir."

Kaen steepled his fingers. "It's been, what, nine years since you joined the Guard?"

"Yes, sir. Coming up on ten in two months."

He nodded. "I can tell you've been around long enough to know when a superior officer is dodging your questions."

No shite. Kira decided a shrug was the best response.

"Well, your observations at the MTech lab support a larger pool of evidence we've gathered over the past eight months. We're at the leading edge of a crisis."

That was surprisingly candid. Kira came to attention. "Sir…?"

"We've been tracking a group of researchers in MTech performing illegal genetic experimentation," Kaen explained. "The lab you infiltrated was one of those facilities, and the data you retrieved is documentation of the experiments."

"What kind of experiments?"

"We believe they are trying to make a hybrid—bringing together the traits of those with telekinetic abilities and some sort of unknown alien physiology."

Kira's mouth involuntarily dropped open. "An… alien hybrid? I didn't know there were—"

"There hasn't been an official first contact with this race, but the information we've received points to an influence outside of known Taran biology. MTech's reports refer to this new group as the 'Robus'."

Alien hybrids with telekinetic abilities? What the fok would a person like that be able to do?! Kira shifted in her chair. "Sir, why are you telling me this?"

"Because we fear that the Mysaran Coalition intends to use these alien-hybrid Robus to attack Elusia, which we anticipate will soon rejoin the Taran Empire. We want to stop that conflict before it starts."

"Of course. But I—"

Kaen fixed her in a level gaze. "The Guard needs you to go back to Valta, Kira. MTech has established a new lab. We need you to find out why."

Kira worked her mouth, unsure what to say. She hadn't been back to her homeworld since she left as a teenager. Her stomach clenched, thinking about what it would be like to return after so long.

While the Guard's promises of using her abilities to help others had resonated with Kira, not everyone in her community had seen it that way. Some considered it a waste of her gift, others an adulteration. Her family had begged her not to leave, but the opportunity to travel the stars was too much for her to pass up. She'd left them all behind—suddenly and without ceremony. She was certain there were lingering hard feelings, even after a decade, and she didn't need that kind of emotional baggage to distract her from a mission. The Guard was her life now.

"Sir, why would MTech set up a lab on Valta?" Even as Kira voiced the question, she already knew the answer. *Whatever gives the planet its special telepathic connections, they want it.*

Mysar and Elusia had argued over claim to Valta since the system was colonized. MTech, though, was a private company and could tread where government could not. However, what Kira had witnessed on MTech's remote moon lab had made it clear that something else was going on besides sanctioned research.

"We trust you'll get to the bottom of it," Kaen responded after giving her a moment to reflect. "You have authorization to use any means necessary."

"No restrictions, sir?" That was a first. Even in the most critical missions, Kira had always been held to strict rules of engagement about which forms of telepathic influence were allowed—a code she followed even in her personal life. If they were granting access to the dark side, the situation was very dire indeed.

Kaen inclined his head. "We need this handled quickly and quietly."

"That's what my team does, sir."

"Your team won't be going with you on this one—at least not for the initial recon work."

Kira's eyes narrowed. "Sir, but—"

"We feel that a more... local contact would be beneficial for the mission." His tone was final.

Kira sighed inwardly. "Of course, sir. I'm happy to work with anyone." She hoped the statement came out with a straight face. In truth, she'd joined the Guard so she'd be among the esteemed elite rather than being partnered with whatever poor sap happened to be assigned to a random project. Her patience for idiots lasted about as long as her tolerance for poor musical accompaniment to viral videos.

"When your name came up for the assignment, our local government contacts remembered you. They located someone with the appropriate qualifications who already appears to be an acquaintance of yours. He'll serve as your liaison."

Just my fantastic luck... Kira braced herself. "Oh, and who's that, sir?"

"Leon Calleti."

Oh, shitebiscuits. "Um."

Kaen raised a quizzical eyebrow.

"That'll be... fine, sir."

Leon Foking Calleti. That figures. It had been more like 'foking Leon Calleti' a decade prior, before Kira dumped him with no notice to join the Guard. Of anyone, he made her the most nervous to see again.

"Excellent. You'll depart on a transport to Valta this afternoon," Kaen stated. "We'll assess the right time to bring in your team once you have the lay of the land."

"Yes, sir." She stood, her head swimming with the possible scenarios for how her reunion with Leon might go.

"Good luck."

"Thank you, sir." *I'm going to need it.*

— — —

It was obvious Kira has been flustered by her partnership with Leon, but Kaen trusted her to adapt. She always did.

With the necessity for Kira's team to be on the sidelines for the first phase, she'd need someone she could trust. An ex, while not ideal, meant an automatic level of familiarity that could never be achieved with a stranger. Couple that with Leon's degree in genetics and he was the perfect counterpart to accompany her in an undercover investigation of the MTech facility on her homeworld.

Kaen turned his attention to his own task: finding the mole in the Guard.

Ever since the official investigation into MTech began

eight months prior, little bits of information hadn't added up—nothing on the scale of the botched mission data for Kira's team, but enough that he'd been suspicious. Now, with the safety of his people and the fate of the Elvar Trinary on the line, they needed to stem the problem. Fast.

He tapped his fingertips together while he thought. *If the mole is working with the Mysarans, we have to bait the trap. What information would a potential opponent want to know?*

An idea popped into his mind. He tried to dismiss it as too risky, but it persisted. Before he could question it further, Kaen touched the comm link icon on his touch-surface desktop. "Cindy, please draft an order for Bravo Company to depart on the *Zepher* tomorrow at 06:00 for a patrol of Mysar's moon. However, do not distribute the communication."

His assistant took a moment to respond. "Sir, I see no prior record of that deployment."

"There hasn't been. Just save it in the public folder—I'll talk to General Lucian."

"Understood, sir. Anything else?"

"No. Thank you, Cindy. Let me know when it's ready." Kaen ended the comm link.

The idea now fully formed, he called up Captain Spencer Thoreau, the outpost's resident digital security specialist. "Captain, I have a favor to ask."

"Whatever you need, Colonel."

"The public folder where we queue deployment orders before the release—can you turn on tracking for everyone who views that folder?"

"Sure," Thoreau replied. "What are you looking for?"

"A pattern. Can you send me a log of the views every hour?"

"Yes, sir, I can set up an automatic report for you."

"Excellent. And is there any chance you can give me access to view the outgoing communications from the facility?"

Thoreau hesitated. "Half of it is classified as personal information. We don't make a point of listening in on conversations between our soldiers and loved ones back home."

"I don't need the content, just the precise data use for any files transferred within the facility and outside."

"Just file size, huh?" The security specialist thought for a moment. "I think I could configure a dashboard for you. Is there something I should be aware of, sir?"

"I'll let you know as soon as I determine that," Kaen told him. "When can you have the dashboard ready?"

"Give me fifteen minutes."

Now that's Guard efficiency. "Thank you, Captain. I'll keep you apprised."

"I'm on it."

No sooner had Kaen ended the comm link than a message from Cindy popped up on his desktop that the mission brief was ready.

He pulled up the file and attached a dummy set of encrypted orders and a manifest—information that would be easier to forward rather than transcribe into a different communication. After closing out of the file, he made a note of the specific file size, then added a tracker to it. Even if the perpetrator stripped away the tracker—as any competent individual would—he'd be able to see if a data packet that size began circulating. Of course, there were no guarantees that the information wouldn't be relayed in some other manner, but the short timeframe would prompt distributing the message to collaborators as quickly as possible.

He leaned back in his chair. *Now we see who bites.*

— — —

Moving into Stage Three so soon wasn't part of the original plan, but Monica Waylon didn't have a choice. With the Tararian Guard closing in, she'd need to do some swift housekeeping.

She strode down the hall with her lab coat fluttering behind her, examining the specimens to either side of the corridor. Early in her career, research subjects had been living, intelligent beings; now they were only tools.

One of the female subjects glared at Monica from inside a cell as she passed, softly glowing green eyes hard with rage. "You can't keep us here. Let us out!"

Monica stopped and pivoted on her heel. It figured that it would be *that* woman to speak up. "We can do whatever we please. You should have read the contract more closely."

"No contract could justify holding innocent civilians captive like this for... stars know how long it's been!"

"Oh, but you're our employees." A devious smile touched Monica's lips. "It's all laid out very clearly in the contract. If the work demands you become permanent residents, then it's within our rights to enforce that clause."

The woman in the cell snarled. "I never signed up to work here!"

"But you chose to immigrate to this world. Like I said, the terms were clearly stated."

"That agreement was two thousand pages long! No one could be expected to read—"

"That's too bad." Monica continued on her way.

Deep down, she knew she was being a heartless bitch, but it was part of the job. When she began working for MTech right out of her graduate program in genetics, a new universe of ethics opened up. No longer was it black and white, good and evil of science and morality, but rather endless shades of gray. To advance, one must push the boundaries of established norms.

Sometimes, testing those boundaries meant inconveniencing a few people. But, for the good of the science and for the Mysaran Coalition, she had a duty to take whatever steps were necessary to achieve the desired ends. In this case, that meant crafting new tools to carry her people into the future.

Monica reached the 'observation room', as they had dubbed the administration center for the underground lab. A series of computer stations were arranged in the center of the room, with monitors mounted to the walls displaying footage of the holding cells and treatment rooms. A door to her right led to the rest of the facility and one on the left provided access to a lab space.

Tim was seated in a rolling chair amidst the central stations. He did a full spin in the chair and stopped, facing her. "Please tell me we get to do something, already. I'm going out of my mind down here."

"Your wish has been granted. We have clearance to proceed with Stage Three."

"About time." Tim did another spin in his chair. "The locals have been asking questions again, you know."

"That doesn't surprise me. They always were a nosy bunch, given how they are."

"It's what makes them so perfect, after all."

Monica examined the other scientist. "Does it ever bother you?"

He raised an eyebrow. "What do you mean?"

"What we're doing here. Permanently changing people's

lives."

He shrugged. "I do think about it sometimes, but my job requires me to remain objective."

"Yes, it does," Monica emphasized. She joined him in the center of the room and activated the control panel, navigating to a video she'd recovered from deleted surveillance footage the night before.

The video popped up on the screen closest to Tim's chair—just a still image of a holding cell, paused on the first frame.

"Now, Tim, I have always valued how you are dedicated to the science. In the five years we've worked together, I have only gained respect for your capabilities as a geneticist. However, for as great as you are with the science, I feel you are equally prone to misplaced sympathies."

"How did you get...?" Tim's face paled. "Monica, I don't know what you saw, but it's not what you think."

"I'm not so sure." Monica's eyes narrowed and she tilted her head, never taking her gaze off of him. "See, if we're moving into Stage Three, I can't have even the slightest hesitation. Everything we've done up to this point will have been child's play by comparison. My team's loyalties must be unquestioned."

Tim sat up straighter in his chair. "Right, of course. You have no reason to doubt me."

"I really wish that were the case." Monica started the video.

Aside from an advancing time-stamp, the video didn't change for several seconds. Then, a woman appeared at the front of the cell—the same woman Monica had confronted several minutes prior. That brief conversation had confirmed what she already knew from the video. Her spirit was alive and well because she had hope for freedom. It could only mean one thing.

Five seconds later, Tim appeared in the frame, rushing toward the cell. "It won't be much longer," he said in the footage.

"I can't take it anymore," the woman pleaded. "Please, just unlock it. I'll find my own way out."

"You'd never make it. Next week—it's all arranged."

She wiped a tear from her face with the heel of her hand. "I guess I'm in no position to argue."

"It'll be okay, Melissa. Trust me."

"I do."

Tim placed his palm against the plexiglass covering the cell entrance, and she held up her own hand to mirror his.

He lingered for two seconds before hurrying away outside the camera's view.

Monica stopped the video, shaking her head with disgust at how easily Tim had lost focus of their mission and fallen to the whims of his heart. It was pitiful.

She glowered over Tim. "I think that's exactly what it looks like."

Her associate rolled backward in his chair. "I can explain—"

"Whatever you were going to say, it's not good enough. I'm sorry, Tim, but with Stage Three coming, you're just too big of a liability. It's a shame." Monica raised her hand.

"No, I—"

Tim's cry cut off in a garbled choke as Monica gripped him in a telekinetic vise, constricting his throat. "For what it's worth, I'll miss you," she told him, his arms flailing as she telekinetically pulled him out of his chair and slowly crushed the life out of him. His eyes lost their fear as they rolled back in his head, his body going limp.

She dropped his body back into the chair. "What a waste," she murmured. Alas, it was so difficult to find good assistants.

CHAPTER 5

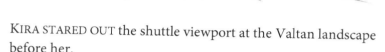

KIRA STARED OUT the shuttle viewport at the Valtan landscape before her.

Pristine mountains rose above a fertile valley, which contained a sprawling forest and a river that wove its way toward the ocean to the east. The unique environmental properties had prompted officials to declare ninety-nine percent of the planet protected land, and her hometown of Tribeca was the largest of only three settlements on the planet.

Due to the covert nature of her mission, she was being dropped off in a civilian shuttle from the orbiting spaceport. Also on board were a group of tourists from Elusia—the obnoxious kind that found obvious features to be the most fascinating thing ever.

The couple across the aisle from Kira was particularly insufferable, making a point of explaining to one another how the hills were different shades of green the farther away they were in the distance. Kira found herself counting prime numbers to keep herself distracted from the inane comments while they landed.

She had just reached three thousand one hundred eighty-seven when the shuttle finally came to rest on the ground.

Across the aisle, the woman pointed out the viewport at a grove of trees along the edge of the landing pad. "Are those, like, parasites?"

"What do you mean?" her husband replied.

She scrunched up her nose. "That white poofy stuff on them. Is it some kind of growth?"

Kira barely resisted smacking her forehead. "Uh, I think that's just a flowering tree."

"Oh, really?" The woman tilted her head. "Huh."

I'm going to strangle her if I don't get off this shuttle right now! Kira unbuckled her harness and quickly grabbed her travel bag before the tourists could make it into the aisle.

The side hatch dropped open, and Kira stepped out.

A warm breeze ruffled her short red hair, and she took a deep breath of the fresh air.

Thanks to the limited number of inhabitants and the strict tourism limitations, the planet was one of the most pristine colonized worlds in the Taran realm. Kira felt fortunate to have grown up in a place with such natural beauty, and it irked her that tourists took it for granted that they could waltz in like they owned the place while meanwhile trashing their own planets. If she had her way, Valta would have much stricter visitation rules—no 'ecotourists' who couldn't identify a flowering tree.

At the bottom of the gangway, Kira paused to assess her surroundings. She had been told someone would come to meet her but had no details beyond that.

No one jumped out at first, but then she spotted him—Leon Calleti. Tall and fit, with sandy hair from his father and mesmerizing violet eyes from his mother, Kira instantly remembered why she'd fallen for him all those years ago.

Thoughts of their time spent together on Valta as teenagers flooded back—begging her to reminisce about simpler times. She tried to ignore the temptation, knowing she couldn't become distracted from her mission. All the same, he was going to make that difficult.

Hoping her face wasn't as flushed as it suddenly felt, she strolled over to Leon and gave a casual nod. "Hey."

"Hi, Kira, it's good to see you." His voice still had just the right timbre.

Snap out of it, Kira! she snarled at herself. *You're a Guard officer. You're better than this.* She took a deep breath and smiled, trying to look the part of the military officer she'd become. "You too, Leon."

"Everyone was pretty surprised to hear you were coming home."

"Yeah, well, I needed a vacation. Not many places better to unplug than here." Her cover story was thin, but it should serve its purpose. While Leon knew the real reason for her visit, it was best to keep up appearances in the public setting.

"Your timing is good. I almost had to leave the planet to find work, but then this new MTech lab opened up."

"That's right, you went to school for genetics. I guess it's 'Dr. Calleti' now, huh?"

Leon's smile enhanced his already luminous eyes. "You should still call me 'Leon'. My position isn't nearly as fancy as it sounds."

Still as humble as ever. Part of Kira had hoped that he'd be bitter or angry with her after how she'd left him, but his poise had been one of the things she'd always found most attractive. She'd realized years before that she'd been in the wrong to leave him how she did, and any ill-will would be well deserved. Seeing him again, still so much like the memories she'd cherished, resurfaced the self-doubt that plagued her in her darkest moments. If she didn't get it in check, she'd have to convince herself all over again that leaving home to join the Guard had been the right move.

"I'm glad everything worked out for you," she replied, just barely meeting his gaze.

"Not much had changed around here since you left, until MTech set up shop. You know how Valta is."

"I do." She looked over the dissipating crowd. "I guess we should get going…"

"Right. I have a car parked at the lot." Leon began strolling toward the small check-in terminal.

"So, how's life?" Kira asked, trying to keep the present moment in perspective. *I'm here for the Guard.*

"My parents are doing well. Ellen moved to Elusia two years ago and hasn't looked back."

"That's right, I do remember her being more of a city girl."

"She's working in politics now, if you can believe it. Last time we talked, she was interviewing for some position on the press staff for the president." Pride filled Leon's voice while he talked about his elder sister.

"That's great!"

He smiled. "Yeah, she was really excited."

They passed by the terminal and entered the small parking lot. Leon headed for a blue two-door vehicle parked in the second row. Its lights flashed as they approached.

"And you—aside from the new job, anything of note?" Kira questioned as she opened the passenger door.

"Not really." Leon shrugged as he slid into the driver's seat. He continued when Kira was seated and doors were closed,

"Since I graduated from my doctoral program on Mysar, I've been focused on getting my career established. I didn't expect to stay here, so I've been keeping to myself."

Is that a roundabout way of letting me know he's single? Kira smoothed her hair behind her ear and secured her seatbelt. "I know what you mean about focusing on career."

Leon placed his hands on the steering wheel but didn't start the vehicle. "Kira, what does the Guard want with this MTech lab?"

"I'm just here to gather information."

"No, you're here to decide what information you want *me* to gather. I want to know what it's for." He stared at her, studying her features as if trying to determine if she'd tell him the truth or not.

"We only want to make sure MTech's work is all above board." At least that was half-true.

"Kira…" He tilted his head questioningly. "This isn't going to work if you're not honest with me."

She stared straight ahead. *I never should have agreed to this mission.* It was under the pretense of hiding her true feelings and intentions that she'd last seen him, and now, a decade later, she was still keeping things from him. "You know the details are classified."

"I won't be able to help you if you don't give me a little more."

Kira finally looked over and met his gaze. "You still want to help me? After everything?"

He slouched in his seat. "You really want to do this now?"

"Not really, no. Honestly, I never thought I'd see you again."

"Well, you're here." There was the bitterness she'd been waiting to hear.

"Yes, I am." She picked at the bottom hem of her shirt. "I'm sorry. I should have said that a long time ago."

He took a slow breath, saying nothing as he stared out the windshield.

"I owe you an explanation—"

"You know, never mind, Kira," Leon cut in. "I don't think *I* want to have this conversation right now. The past is the past. Let's focus on this MTech situation." He started the car.

"Yeah. Okay." She gathered herself. *The mission. Stay focused on the mission.*

"So, what are you after?" he prompted while pulling out of the parking space.

She sighed. "All right. We recently investigated another MTech operation that was… questionable. We're concerned that this facility might be working on that same project, and I need you to use your position at the lab to get me in as a visitor so I can check it out."

Understanding passed across his face. "Right, and they sent you because of your unique gifts in the information-gathering department."

"Being a native was part of it, yeah."

"Well, I'll tell you right now, I don't have access to most of the lab. They have all the operations compartmentalized, and clearance to different areas goes along with that."

"I can find my way," she assured him.

He sat in silence for several seconds. "What happens if your suspicions are confirmed?"

"My team comes in and we shut it down."

"This is MTech, Kira. They won't take kindly to the Guard showing up at their door."

"We'll bust the door down whether they invite us in or not."

He shook his head. "You never used to think about things

that way."

"A lot has changed."

"I guess people do go in different directions, like you said when we last saw each other." Leon directed the car toward the road leading away from the port.

A sharp pang struck her heart. "I couldn't stay here and just be a Reader, making a living off tourist tips."

"I get that, but there were other—"

"The Guard has been good for me, Leon. I don't have regrets."

He focused on the road ahead. "Good."

Kira bit her lip. Even without glimpsing his mind, she could tell Leon still had a flame burning for her even after all this time. That really wasn't what she needed to hear. Despite what she said, she did regret never letting the relationship run its natural course. No one she'd met in the Guard came close to what they'd had together. But as much as she wished they could rekindle that romance, they were in different worlds now, despite this brief intersection.

She set the thoughts aside. She had a job to do. "I'm feeling antsy after being cooped up on the civilian transport ship. Do you know a good gym?"

"As a matter of fact, I've taken up Fizic Proma. You're welcome to come with me later."

"I never pegged you as one to get into martial arts."

He shrugged. "I'm not the same person I used to be, either."

Kira eyed him. "All right. I'll see what you're made of."

Leon cracked a smile. "I think I might even be able to show a Guard soldier a thing or two."

— — —

The capitol building for the Elusian government rose above the surrounding city, its gleaming metal façade and blue glass reflecting the afternoon sun. From her office on the seventh floor, Ellen Calleti was able to see the bottom portion of the tapered structure, sloping down into the enclosed garden surrounding the base of the building. It all seemed so shiny and pristine from up here, but over the last two years on Elusia, she'd learned the inner workings of government were anything but.

Ellen tucked a loose strand of sandy hair behind her ear and tapped her stylus against her touch-surface desktop, thinking through the implications of the latest message in her personal email: >>*The next phase has begun. Be ready.*<<

She had been ready since the day she left Valta. Everything she'd done had led to the position she now held, giving her access to the most senior members of the Elusian government. That position placed her in the center of powerful political machinations with opposing goals.

On the one hand, the Taran Empire offered a measure of political stability and access to resources unlike anything her people had ever seen. Rejoining as a full member of the Empire would mean her people would want for nothing.

However, the Elusian Alliance and its frenemy neighbor, the Mysaran Coalition, disagreed about what their place would be in the Taran Empire. The Elusians were all for reunification, but a growing number of Mysarans favored complete independence. A shared economy between the planets meant that only one world joining would disrupt the balance for everyone in the Elvar Trinary.

As far as Ellen was concerned, continued independence was worth that temporary upset.

She knew what would happen if transit between worlds became open to all—how her beautiful home of Valta would be overrun by tourists and Empire scientists seeking to exploit the planet in the name of scientific research. Beyond that, she couldn't trust that a galactic entity like the Taran Empire would have any respect for a little three-planet system like her home. Her people would be swallowed up and exploited.

They would be better off if the Elvar Trinary was on its own. The only obstacle was Elusia.

An incoming voice-only call lit up on Ellen's desktop. The caller's details were marked only as 'Unknown'. She knew exactly who it must be.

She answered. "You shouldn't be contacting me at my office like this."

"It is almost time for action. Are you ready?" the digitally distorted voice replied.

"Of course. But I thought the next phase was still months away?"

"We decided an expedited approach was needed. The details aren't important."

Ellen frowned. Her collaborators *never* seemed keen on sharing the details. Until she pressed. "What does this next phase entail?"

"A deliverable that isn't your concern."

"But what—"

"You must play your part," the voice cut her off. "Can we count on you?"

Her face flushed, and she took a deep breath. "Yes."

The call disconnected.

Ellen wiped her sweaty palms on her gray pencil skirt. Her role was critical, and she knew her people were counting on her. One day soon, she would kill the President of the Elusian

Alliance.

— — —

Data could lie, but the story these particular forensics told might just be twisted enough to be true.

Kaen evaluated the trail left by his dummy file. He had anticipated the file would be relayed directly from the Guard servers to some outside recipient, likely in the Mysaran Coalition. However, not one but *four* individuals had viewed the file and then subsequently forwarded it on.

One of the forwards was a legitimate fleet order, so Kaen dismissed it. *The other three, though...* He was up against more than just one collaborator, and it was obvious from the transmittal records that it was not toward the same ends. The test he'd designed was a little *too* enticing. He may have inadvertently accelerated a civil war.

Shite! Why now? The Elusian Alliance had been so close to signing the official reunification agreement with the Taran Empire. He needed to come clean so they could get ahead of the situation—if that was even possible.

Kaen grunted his frustration as he pulled up the contact details for the Elusian president.

Elton Joris answered almost immediately. "Colonel Kaen, I didn't expect a call so soon."

"I'm sorry to bother you again, Mr. President, but my investigation has taken an unexpected turn."

"Oh?"

"I'm afraid the leak isn't isolated to someone in the Guard feeding information to the Mysarans. It appears that there's a collaborator in your very administration, and that individual is connected to a contact in one of the major news outlets."

The president frowned, the flush in his face making his hair appear even whiter. "What would be gained from that?"

"Indirect control. If the Guard needs to take military action, our stealth movements could be preempted with a public news article. It's a great way to control what we can do—stay quiet when our movements are beneficial for their agenda, or expose us if it's not in their interest."

"There have to be more effective ways to intervene."

"Yes, but by adding a public disclosure component, they gain significant leverage."

Joris considered the argument. "That means someone might be writing an article right now."

Kaen took an unsteady breath. "Yes, sir, and it won't tell a good story."

"Why, what bait did you use?"

"For a fleet to mobilize at Mysar's moon."

"Fok!" The president turned away from the camera and shook his head. He breathed out through his teeth and then turned back. "How bad is it?"

"That depends on how closely someone looks. The orders were never officially signed off by General Lucian. However, if someone is interested in sensationalized news media, that detail is probably irrelevant."

"Well, that's just foking great." The president rubbed his eyes.

"I apologize, sir. I didn't anticipate this contingency when I designed my test. The intent was to see if Mysar mobilized a military response for a fleet that wouldn't be there. But if this false information becomes public, they'd declare that the Guard is making a decisive military move."

"Just when I thought things couldn't get any worse…" Joris paced in front of the camera. "Someone in my own administration could bring the entire agreement with the Taran Empire crashing down."

"I've pulled the document and issued a cancellation."

The president groaned. "That doesn't matter. If someone wants to use those original orders against us from the inside, they'll do it. People only look at headlines, so real fleet or not, we'd be facing an unchecked outcry of public opinion on how to handle the situation."

Kaen hung his head. "I'm sorry, sir. I never thought we'd have to worry about anything on the Elusian side."

"Neither did I." He sighed. "I'll need to make a statement. We can't have public opinion questioning the vassal agreement at this late stage."

"In better news, the test was successful. I know where the leaks are, so this won't be an issue in the future," Kaen offered.

"Assuming those are the only leaks."

One step at a time. "Yes."

"Fix this." The president ended the call.

Kaen slumped back in his chair. *This went sideways at record speed...*

His worst nightmare escalated to a whole new level when an incoming communication request illuminated on his desktop. General Lucian was calling. *Oh, fok.*

CHAPTER 6

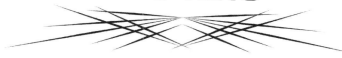

KIRA'S HOMETOWN OF Tribeca had grown since she left, but it had retained the quaint charm of stucco building finishes and extensive greenspace even within the urban center.

She and Leon chatted as they drove, falling into a comfortable rhythm once the initial tension dissipated. Though the issues from their unresolved past would no doubt come up again, she embraced the opportunity to catch up with Leon as a longtime friend.

Their destination was a new residential suburb located next to the recently constructed MTech lab. The residential neighborhood consisted of compact one- to two-bedroom cottages that shared common outdoor space.

"Only about half the homes are occupied so far," Leon explained as he pulled up in front of a cottage in the middle of the development. "I reserved one for you near mine so we can debrief more easily."

"Great, thanks." Kira stepped out of the car and stretched while taking in her surroundings. The grounds around the cottage were landscaped with long-stalked red flowers, and the lawn wrapped around a central fire pit and patio area. "It's beautiful here."

"Sure beats those tin cans you live in."

Kira frowned. "You might be surprised how nice some ships are."

"And those luxury yachts are what you travel around in with the Guard?"

"That's beside the point."

Leon chuckled. "Thought so."

She retrieved her travel bag from the car's trunk and followed Leon to the cottage's entrance.

Leon unlocked it with a keycard and handed it to her. "Home sweet home," he said.

"No biometric lock?" she questioned.

"We use keycards at the lab, too. Easier to visually check from a distance."

Kira shrugged. "Whatever works."

She peeked inside the cottage. The compact living room contained a couch, entertainment center, and a kitchenette. Doors adjacent to the kitchenette led to a bathroom and a bedroom. "This looks good, thanks. I shouldn't be here long."

"Why do I have a sneaking suspicion that when you're done with this investigation, I'm going to be out of a job?"

Kira leaned against the doorframe. "I hope that's not the case, but I'll do anything I can to help you find another position if it comes to that."

"I'm not worried about finding other employment. I'd just hate to think that I was a part of something that was in some way dangerous or harmful."

"In my time in the Guard, I've learned corruption has many layers. Even if one MTech lab is up to no good, that doesn't mean the organization as a whole is bad, or that people who work for them are enemies. A small handful of people can set the tone for much larger issues."

"So you think whatever is going on here is an offshoot of the organization?"

"We'll know soon enough," she replied. "But, Leon... I need to know that you'll share everything you discover with me, even if it's unfavorable. If I find something that's not right, can I count on you to help me do whatever needs to be done—shut down the lab, file documents with the Mysaran government, whatever?"

He searched her face. "I'll do what I think is in the best interest of Valta."

"Then I think we should be on the same page." She nodded.

He cracked a smile. "I'm looking forward to seeing you at work. You always enjoyed a challenging investigation."

"This is a little different from a school research paper," Kira replied with a smirk.

"Everything is always more fun when up against a shady organization with interstellar security on the line."

"Let's not go too far! It may be nothing."

Leon crossed his arms. "Kira, we both know you wouldn't be here if it were 'nothing'. You're here because there's already an issue."

She looked down. "And that's why they picked you to be the local contact. Not much makes it past you."

"Which is why it's so surprising to hear that MTech may be up to something. In the two months I've been at the lab, everything has seemed completely legit."

"It often does," Kira murmured.

"But if it's not, I want to know. And I want to make things right. This is my community—the last thing I want is for there to be a poison in our midst."

She nodded and gazed into his violet eyes. "That's why I joined the Guard. I wanted to root out the bad and make things better. Just so happens that the scale of those assignments goes beyond the scope of one city or planet."

"I get it." He looked like he was about to say something else, but then he took a step back. "I'll let you get settled in. I told the lab I'd head over in a couple of hours to check on the progress of some analyses, and you can tag along."

"Ah, the 'old friend visiting from out-of-town' routine."

"The very one." Leon looked her over one more time. "See you at 15:00."

Kira watched him enter a cottage two away from hers. She stepped the rest of the way into her own residence and closed the door, dropping her bag on the ground.

The upcoming visit to the lab should help to fill in the gaps in the narrative running through her mind. *What is MTech after? Who are they working for?* With any luck, the answers would be straightforward.

She chuckled to herself, knowing better. There were no easy answers.

— — —

Not surprisingly, General Lucian had ripped Kaen a new one for posting unendorsed deployment orders. Kaen was still reeling from the conversation, but he'd gotten out of it with his rank and most of his dignity intact.

After he'd explained the reasoning behind his approach to rooting out the mole, the general had seen fit to let him correct the issue himself—good intentions, and all that. All the same, he was on notice. He needed to address the known leaks and make sure that any other as-yet-undiscovered collaborators would have a difficult time relaying anything useful in the future.

Kaen's first task would be to meet with the head of the Guard outpost's security, Major Deanna Olvera. Given the tricky situation, he had to make sure the events unfolded in the proper sequence.

He took the elevator down one level to the security division's main operations center and strode toward Olvera's office, across the lobby filled with surveillance screens. She was absorbed in an image on her monitor when Kaen knocked on the doorframe.

Olvera looked up, startled. "Oh, hello, Colonel. What can I do for you?"

"It's urgent, and it's more than a quick conversation," he replied.

"Have a seat." She gestured to the single chair in the front corner of the room.

Kaen closed the office door and dragged the chair up to her desk. "We have a leak. Well, actually three that I know about."

"This have anything to do with that monitoring dashboard Captain Thoreau set up for you?"

"You know about that?"

"I'd be a pretty terrible head of security if I didn't recognize a trap when I saw one, sir." Olvera cracked a slight smile. "So, who took the bait?"

"No one I know personally, though their names and faces are familiar. I checked their personnel records and there were no red flags before this incident. A low-level comm officer, a lieutenant with one of our special ops teams, and a captain assigned to security oversight."

Olvera's brow furrowed. "What's the captain's name?"

"Samuel Ellis."

"Sam? That's…" Her voice faded out. "He's never given me any reason to doubt him."

Kaen leaned over the desktop and placed his right palm flat against the surface. When a prompt appeared, he entered his password to log into the system. He navigated to the record of the data packet's transfer. "You can see Ellis' access of the file here—a document he'd have no reason to open. The tracker was stripped, but if you note the file size, you can see an exact matching document was forwarded from Ellis' account to a server in Mysaran territory four hours ago."

"I can't argue with the evidence, but I don't understand why he'd do this," Olvera said.

"I have a hunch, though it would make things even more complicated if I'm right."

"What is it?"

"That these three incidents are independent of one another. Multiple forces are at work toward different ends."

Olvera's frown deepened. "Why do you suspect that?"

"Because the recipients of these data packets are so diverse: a media outlet on Elusia, the Mysaran military, and the new MTech lab on Valta."

"What if they *are* connected?" Olvera speculated.

"Then I have no idea what the endgame might be."

She nodded. "Only way to find out is to detain each of them for questioning. If there's a link, we'll find it."

CHAPTER 7

AFTER A SHORT nap on the couch, Kira awoke with a clear mind, feeling refreshed. The air and unique energy on Valta always had a revitalizing effect, and it was only after a decade away that she realized just how much she'd missed it.

She took a shower to wash off the travel residue and changed into a dress. A girly dress—with a flower print. She hadn't worn anything but a military uniform or powered armor in... she couldn't even remember how long.

Kira blow-dried and styled her short hair. It wasn't until she saw herself in the dress that she missed the long hair she'd sported in her pre-Guard days. But long, flowing hair had no place in uniform when she needed to cram her head into tight helmets. Her pixie cut was pushing the boundaries of regulation as it was.

Maybe one day... she thought wistfully. *Whoa, where did that come from?*

Being back home wasn't off to a good start.

She hurriedly finished dressing and stepped outside to get

some fresh air while she waited for Leon to come over. The afternoon sun warmed her face as she faced it with her eyes closed, slowly rotating her arms to get even exposure.

"I bet I can find you a lounge chair," Leon's voice interrupted her sunning.

Kira's eyes shot open. "I don't think I'll have much time for relaxing. Figured I should get in a few seconds while I could."

"Well, you *are* supposed to be here for some R&R," he pointed out. "I'm just trying to help you look the part." He grinned.

"You always were good at bending the rules."

"Me? I'm very by-the-book."

"Uh huh, says the person who calculated a weighted average of all assignments in his classes to figure out the bare minimum score necessary on the final to get an 'A' in the class."

Leon shrugged. "That was just efficiency."

"Rule-bender."

"Efficiency-hater," he shot back with a daring grin.

She laughed. *After all these years, the repartee is alive and well.* As much as she wanted to needle him further, there was no point in starting something she knew she couldn't finish. "I guess we should get you back to the lab."

"Right." He headed for the car. "You look really nice, by the way."

Kira looked down at herself. "Thanks. Hopefully I don't need to rearrange anyone's face today, because these shoes are a far cry from combat boots, and I am not sure if blood would come out of this dress' fabric."

"If you need to do that, then I don't think your undercover op would be off to a very good start."

"You bring up a valid point." Kira climbed into the car and buckled her seatbelt. "To that end, what should I know about this place?"

Leon focused out the windshield and started the engine. "I feel like you'll ignore everything I have to say."

"Try me."

He sighed and pulled out of the driveway onto the road. "It's all pretty standard. Most workers, like me, started about two months ago, after construction was complete. MTech brought in their own construction crew from offworld as well as their own senior management. There's a front reception area and, as far as I can tell, three wings to the facility. I work in the A Wing, which is to the right when you enter through the lobby. We have an administrative area with computers for data processing, a cafeteria, and there are some private rooms for interviews, medical procedures, and the like."

"What kind of medical procedures?" Kira prompted.

"Minor tissue samples, mostly. As a geneticist, I'll occasionally work with a specific subject. All we need is a cheek swab, but it sets the patients at ease to have a room that looks official."

"I could see that."

"As for the B and C Wings, they're devoted to nanotech research and biomedical engineering, respectively."

Sounds suspiciously similar to what we encountered in that moon lab... "Anything else beyond those three areas?"

"Not that I know of, but I can't definitively rule out the possibility."

"In that case, there's almost *certainly* something else, especially considering that they went out of their way to bring in their own construction crew."

"Based on what little you've told me, that's sounding more and more likely."

"What about the staff?" Kira asked.

"Handful of locals like me," Leon replied, "paired with the MTech corporate senior managers, and some specialists from various academic institutions."

"Anyone of note?"

"I haven't met him personally, but I heard there's a pretty well-known nano researcher over in B Wing who specializes in biomedical applications."

That sounds about right. Kira sighed. "I don't suppose you have clearance to access that area?"

"No, but I can at least get you a visitor tour of A Wing where I work."

Kira clasped her hands. "Leon, you're the best."

"The Guard better be standing by for an evac in case this goes south."

"Don't worry, they'll have our backs. As long as you stick with me, you're golden."

They drove the rest of the way to the facility in virtual silence, though Kira made occasional comments about new developments along the road that hadn't been there when she'd last seen her home city.

The MTech lab itself was set into a hillside of the valley containing the city of Tribeca. From the outside, it looked to be only a one-story structure, with a white stone façade and tinted glass that reflected the afternoon sun. Half a dozen armed guards were stationed out front, and the roof featured a remote-operated gun.

"Um, Leon… You didn't tell me about the gun mounted outside to welcome your visitors."

"Oh, right. I guess I've gotten used to it."

Kira smoothed her dress with her hands. "Leon, a giant assault gun is not a normal thing to have above the main entrance to a civilian research facility."

"Yeah, that was a little unnerving at first…"

"'Unnerving'?! Are you serious? This is insane!" Kira exclaimed. She took a deep breath. She looked back over at her companion with a more level expression. "This just means I might need to get more creative than I'd initially anticipated."

"I have no doubt you'll manage." Leon parked the car in a marked employee lot to the left of the main driveway.

The parking lot was situated in an open field at the base of the hill housing the lab facility. Several boulders embedded in the surrounding field had been arranged to form the entry for the lot, and a path wove around the edge of a circular drive leading up to the entrance.

Leon turned off the car, and they stepped out.

"Now, who am I again?" Kira prompted, testing that Leon would default to her cover story.

"A childhood friend. You're on leave from the Guard after a challenging op and are looking to reconnect with your homeland so you can re-find yourself."

She shrugged. "Close enough. Lead the way, buddy ol' pal."

He rolled his eyes at her and proceeded down the path to the lab's entrance.

As they approached, the guards out front stiffened.

Leon held out his ID badge. "Returning from a long lunch. A friend of mine is in from out-of-town; I'll check her in at reception."

The guard closest to them nodded and waved them through without the slightest break in his permanent scowl.

"Really went all out on the welcoming committee," Kira commented once they were beyond earshot.

"Believe it or not, he's way more charismatic than the last guy."

Kira scanned around the overhang above the entrance

while she passed underneath, noting a full suite of optical and thermal sensors. If that was any indication, there would be a host of additional equipment hidden within. She'd need to have a legitimate reason to come back—one that would afford her some freedom.

Leon approached the reception desk that stood a dozen paces inside. He smiled at the cute blonde behind it. "Hi, Martha. My friend Kira here is visiting for the week, and I was hoping to show off my new digs. Could you help me out with a visitor pass?"

Martha looked Kira over. "We have a strict visitation policy—"

"Is there *anything* you can do? I'll stay with her the whole time, and just in the general access areas."

"Really, I just want to see if the lunch room is as nice as he tells me it is." Kira winked. She brushed her hand against Leon's arm; his bicep was as firm as it looked through his shirt. *Focus on the mission.*

Martha glanced down at her desk. "We do have a special friends and family pass, but you'll need to check out by 17:00."

"More than enough time," Leon said with a bright smile. "Just you wait and see about that lunch room," he teased Kira.

"Yeah, yeah." She gave a playful roll of her eyes.

"You two are just too cute." Martha giggled. "Now—Kira, was it? I'll just need your palm print on this panel and a quick photo to get you your ID."

Great, my biometrics logged into their private database. So much for sneaking around and not leaving a trace. She plastered on her best fake smile. "Great, no problem." She placed her hand on the designated panel atop the reception desk and looked into the indicated camera for her glamour shot.

"Perfect." Martha made some entries on her keyboard.

"And I'll just need you to sign this waiver."

Text appeared on the desktop in front of Kira. "What does it entail?"

"I'm sure it's nothing," Leon whispered.

Undercover op or not, I'm not signing away my body to science if they're trying to pull some shady shite. She scanned over the agreement. It wasn't quite handing over her soul, but it was close. "This is quite the agreement, Martha."

"I'm afraid agreeing to those terms is necessary for me to issue a visitor badge," the receptionist replied.

Fok, I guess handing over my body is what I did when I signed up for the Guard, anyway. Kira placed her thumbprint on the appropriate box for her digital signature, and the screen turned blue.

"Great, we're all set. Just one second." Martha swiveled around and grabbed an ID card printing from a machine on the shelf behind her. She scooted back to her desk and handed the badge to Kira. "Now, don't lose this. Be sure to return it to me when you're done with your tour."

Kira clipped the badge to the front of her dress. "You've got it, Martha. Thanks for your help."

"Enjoy your time!"

Leon headed toward a security archway to the right. He flashed his badge at the guard standing next to the arch and was beckoned through.

Kira smiled at the guard while she pointed to her badge and followed Leon.

The guard held up his hand to stop her. "Please remove the ID card and hand it to me, miss."

Yep, definitely not waltzing in here without an express invitation. Remaining calm, she did as she was told.

The guard studied the ID and consulted a hidden monitor

on a kiosk in front of him. "Says here you're active duty Tararian Guard."

"On personal leave at the moment," Kira replied.

"No foreign military is allowed into the facility."

Kira glanced at Leon. "Oh, come now. We'll all be part of the Empire soon enough, right?"

"They issued her credentials. The system would have flagged her if it was a problem," Leon interjected.

"You a native of Valta?" the guard asked Kira.

"I am."

"Ah, that's it. Locals are an exception."

She breathed an inward sigh of relief. "I'm excited to see what new industry has come to my hometown," she said with a cheery tone to mask the sarcasm behind her words.

"Enjoy your visit." The guard handed back her badge.

"Thanks, have a good afternoon." Kira stepped through the archway after Leon.

They passed through a secured entry and entered a white hallway lined with doors.

"That was more intense than I expected," Kira said as soon as the outer door was closed.

"Lots of IP in there. Just want to make sure nothing walks out that's not supposed to," Leon replied. An upward shift in his eyes indicated that he was filtering his response for the benefit of the surveillance system.

"I appreciate their dedication."

Leon picked up his pace. "It's a top-notch group."

"You're just saying that because you work here," Kira jested.

"Hey, I never said the opinion wasn't biased." He winked at her.

"Yeah, whatever. Get this tour going."

Leon led her down the hall to an intersection and took a left. The hall opened into a common room filled with round tables. A buffet line was set up along the back wall, and along the right wall was an expansive screen depicting nature images ranging from majestic landscapes to little fuzzy critters.

He held out his arm in grand fashion. "I present to you… the cafeteria."

Kira had made up the lunch room ruse at the front desk, but she did have to admit the cafeteria beat the mess hall at Orion Station hands down. "All right, I'm impressed."

"But I know what you really wanted to see was my workspace." Leon crossed the cafeteria, heading for a door on the opposite wall.

"Just curious how you spend your day," she replied for the camera's benefit. *And getting some time on the network wouldn't be all bad…*

After a brief walk down the hall beyond the cafeteria, the corridor terminated in an open space filled with workstations. A dozen individuals were scattered around the room, and they looked up with curious expressions when Kira entered.

"Everyone, this is Kira," Leon introduced. "She's an old friend of mine. We grew up together."

"Oh, another Valtan native?" a thin man with dark complexion commented from a nearby station.

"Yeah, I am," Kira replied.

"You have any of those special gifts everyone's always talking about?" he asked.

"She does," Leon replied before Kira had a chance to stop him.

"Really?" the man's eyes widened. "What can you do?"

"Oh, nothing too special," Kira replied, casting a silencing glare toward Leon.

"A Reader, huh?" a musical female voice said from across the room. "Now that's something I have yet to experience."

"Dr. Waylon!" Leon's face flushed. "I wasn't expecting to see you over here."

"You know how I like to make the rounds." The brown-haired woman fixed her gaze on Kira. "Who's your friend?"

"Kira, ma'am," she replied. "And you are…?"

"Monica Waylon. You might consider me the director of this facility."

"Well, it's a lovely place you have here," Kira said. "I can't believe how much has changed since I was last in Tribeca."

"MTech always hopes to leave a positive impact on our communities," Monica responded with a too-sweet smile. "I've been so curious about the abilities of the native population here."

"We're not exactly *native*," Kira corrected. "Our people colonized here the same time as the other Taran-occupied worlds in this sector."

"Of course. And that makes it all the more fascinating that you so rapidly developed your unique telepathic abilities." She folded her hands in front of her. "How old were you when your gifts emerged?"

Kira shrugged. "Around eight."

"That's young, isn't it? You must be very talented."

"There isn't necessarily a link between the age when abilities emerge and their strength," Kira said, skirting the truth. While it wasn't always linked, in her case that had very much been the reality. Whereas the average age for a first Reading came around twelve, the early emergence of abilities had given her extra time with the elders to learn and study the craft.

Had she stayed with them, she likely would have been the

most powerful Reader in two generations.

"I didn't mean to imply," Monica said in that sickeningly sweet tone. "You must forgive me—I've never had the chance to meet anyone of your talents before."

"Oh, I'm sure you've met far more interesting people than me." Kira took a subconscious step back and instinctually bolstered her mental guards.

"We were in the middle of our tour, ma'am," Leon said, seeming to pick up on Kira's discomfort. "We have to be out of here by 17:00."

"Nonsense. We wouldn't be here without the support of the Valtans," Monica replied. "Kira, you're welcome any time."

"That's very generous of you, ma'am. Thank you."

"In fact," the director continued, "I'd love to have the chance to meet with you in a more formal capacity."

The question caught Kira off-guard. "Uh… Well, I'm here on vacation, actually."

"I'd compensate you for your time, of course. I'd just like to better understand how you do what you can do."

The last thing I need is the director of this freakshow tracking my every move. Kira gave a polite bow of her head. "I appreciate your interest, but I'm—"

"That's a generous offer, Dr. Waylon," Leon cut in. "I think that might be just what Kira needs to reconnect with herself. That is why you came back here, right?" he asked while turning toward her.

Kira resisted the urge to punch him in that gorgeous jaw of his. "Yes, just what I need," she responded to him tightly, and returned her focus to the director. "Thank you, Dr. Waylon."

"Call me Monica, please." She flashed a smile bordering on predatory. "Come in with Leon tomorrow morning and we'll get to know each other."

"Can't wait."

"If you'll excuse me." Monica passed by them with a nod of farewell and disappeared into the hall.

Kira glared at Leon and mouthed, "The fok...?"

He took her by the arm and led her toward a private office. "Now, Kira, aren't you looking forward to being a guest in this facility? You'll get to see so much more of it."

"Yes, right alongside the director."

"Dr. Waylon is very busy, unfortunately. I doubt she'll be able to spend all her time with you."

Kira caught on. *And might leave me unattended in a place I couldn't access otherwise.* There were no guarantees, but it was worth a shot. She chose her words carefully in case anyone was listening in. "I look forward to whatever time with her I can get."

Leon looked around the room. "So, anyway, this is my office."

The room was approximately three meters square and contained a desk, a holographic workboard, and two visitor chairs.

"It's nice." Kira eyed the desk. "I bet with a setup like this, you don't have to leave to access all the files you might need for a project."

"My login is restricted, of course, but the facility is networked."

What I wouldn't give to have Nia or Kyle here right now, Kira lamented. Her own hacking skills were nothing to dismiss, but her Guard teammates were the real masters. She only nodded in response.

Leon waved her forward. "Come on, let's finish the tour."

— — —

Monica smiled to herself as she walked away from the lab's latest visitor. In all her research, she hadn't had access to someone of Kira's talents; it was the one gap in her otherwise rigorous exercise of the scientific method. With all the potential knowledge to be gained, Kira might be someone worthy of Monica's attention.

She strolled to her office deep within the facility—down in the secret D Wing only a select few knew how to access. Monica had overseen the design and construction personally to make sure it fulfilled her vision.

The observation room only had a single occupant: a brown-haired man named Jared who had replaced Tim after his unfortunate 'accident'.

"Jared," Monica addressed as she walked through the room, "I'd like you to look into a new visitor for me."

"Who, ma'am?"

"First name is 'Kira'. You should be able to find out the rest from her records at the front desk."

Jared made several entries on his monitor. "Full name is Kira Elsar. According to her public biodata records, she's an active duty captain in the Tararian Guard."

Monica nodded thoughtfully. "Does it say anything about her past assignments?"

"No, sorry, ma'am. There's a note that she's on leave at the moment, but otherwise the details of her service records are classified."

"Of course. Anyone working in military intelligence can't have their mission history out there on display."

"Would you like me to look into her?" Jared offered.

Monica shook her head. "It doesn't take much speculation to figure out what a telepath with the Guard might specialize in."

Jared's eyes lit up. "Oh, she's one of the Readers?"

"So I've heard. A Valtan Reader with specialized military training."

A slow smile spread across the other scientist's face. "That makes things interesting."

"It does, doesn't it?" Monica had a feeling Jared was going to work out much better than his predecessor. "Keep an eye on her. I believe we've been handed the perfect case study."

"I will." Jared paused. "And what about that information regarding the Guard mobilization around Mysar?"

"Don't worry about that. Focus on our task at hand. Our benefactors won't wait much longer."

She moseyed across the observation room to the corridor containing the holding cells for her test subjects.

The one hundred subjects with innate telekinetic abilities had taken years and significant resources to apprehend, but studying their genetic profiles had given Monica the breakthrough she needed to begin customizing the alien nanotech at the core of their research. Coupled with the technical specifications furnished by her outside collaborators, she had been able to drill down to the base level of nanite programming and design.

Monica approached the front plexiglass wall of Melissa's cell—the spirited woman who would have had Tim free her and unleash the unstable nanotech into the universe. "How are you feeling today?"

Melissa glared back from her cot. "Where's Tim? I know you found out about us."

"I'm afraid Tim no longer works here."

"What did you do to him?!" Melissa launched toward the plexiglass. Her nails had transformed into silvery claws by the time she struck her hands against the transparent wall. Her eyes raged orange, the natural bioluminescent glow of her innate telekinetic abilities augmented by the effects of the experimental nanites.

"I killed him with my bare hands."

Melissa raked her claws against the glass. "I'll foking kill you, bitch!" The words were barely intelligible.

"He didn't even put up a fight."

A silvery sheen covered Melissa's pale skin as nanites flooded out from inside her to begin transforming her into a hybrid alien state. The metallic film thickened into scales, which broadened her shoulders and limbs, ripping the pale gown that clothed her. She howled in agony, her claws tearing ribbons from the white plastic sheeting around the cell. Her movements accelerated—fast, precise, vicious.

Monica observed the Robus' movements, a pleased smile curling her lips. The fluidity and deadly force was a more perfect hybrid of abilities than she could have ever hoped to achieve.

After two minutes of struggling, Melissa collapsed to the floor panting. She returned to her standard state, her gown torn around the neck.

"Thank you for the demonstration. It was quite enlightening." Monica turned from the glass. "You'll be reunited with your Tim soon enough."

CHAPTER 8

WHAT IN THE stars is the Guard up to? The classified fleet orders that had passed over Ellen's desk on the way to her media contact had left her confused and worried. There wasn't supposed to be any military action against the Mysarans—at least, not yet.

She drummed her fingers on her desktop, trying to predict what would happen next.

With the trade negotiations to rejoin the Taran Empire in full swing, any political or military move would be magnified—it's what they had been counting on with Ellen's placement in the president's office—but any unanticipated actions also threatened their plans. The timing needed to be right.

The shared history of Mysarans and Elusians forever tied the two groups together, tracing back to when the worlds had been settled hundreds of years prior. With the Elusians committed to rejoining the Empire, the Mysarans had little choice other than to go along for the ride—unless they took drastic action.

Ellen's role would accomplish that—a presidential assassination staged to look like a betrayal by the Empire. If handled correctly, it would be enough to reverse the discussions and guarantee the system's independence. However, that groundwork would all be undone if the Empire wiped out Mysar before Elusia had a chance to withdraw from the reunification agreement.

Ellen knew how much was riding on her, but the latest development with Guard activity could make all of her preparations moot. A Tararian Guard move against the Mysarans meant that Elusia and Mysar were no longer being treated as an inseparable pair—one was now on its way into the Empire, and the other was out. If the Mysarans were left on their own… it wouldn't go well.

Uncertainty got the better of her, and she sent an encrypted message to her anonymous contact: >>*Does this change the timeline?*<<

The reply came back a minute later: >>*We will let you know when to act.*<<

She bit back her frustration.

"Ellen Calleti," the voice over the intercom interrupted her brooding. "Your services are needed in the president's office."

Her heart leaped. *They just told me to wait!* Then she remembered her place and the other job she was there to do. "On my way," she replied.

Ellen grabbed her tablet and hurried from her office.

She took the elevator up two floors to the president's suite, swiping her hand over the biometric lock. In seconds, the doors opened to a lobby floored with marble. Holographic overlays of news reports scrolled across the left wall. To the right, a slim young man sat at a reception desk.

"Hi, Nico," Ellen greeted. "The president wanted to see

me?"

"Yes, go right in."

Ellen took a steadying breath and walked straight ahead to the double-doors, passing by two security guards dressed in black. They nodded to her.

She rapped on the door.

"Come in."

Swinging the door inward, Ellen composed her face in a polite smile. "How may I assist you, Mr. President?" She closed the door behind her.

The roomy office had windows looking out over the city and the ice-filled river along the southern border. Afternoon winter sun cast long shadows across the icy landscape, illuminating the city in an uncharacteristically warm glow. The reflecting light gave the president a vibrant appearance, which was at odds in Ellen's mind with her knowledge of his imminent death.

"I need to prepare a statement," President Joris replied.

Ellen activated her tablet. "Subject, sir?"

"That bomaxed information leak about the Guard making a move on Mysar."

"What do you mean, sir? I thought—"

"Those weren't genuine orders," the president grunted. "A foking colossal miscommunication."

It went without saying that particular phrasing wouldn't make it into the press release. "How do you want to play this, sir?"

Ellen would need to put her own spin on it, regardless of what was released in the official statement. Someone had intentionally fed her false information. *If that wasn't genuine, how much else has been doctored?*

She swallowed and gripped her stylus tighter.

President Joris stroked his chin. "We need to look unified. The Elusians and Mysarans settled our homeworlds at the same time, and we are bound to each other. We must stand by one another and approach the future with our mutual interests at the forefront. Though we have not always agreed on every matter, we have made great strides toward establishing that shared vision for a better future. With the opportunity to strengthen our great nations by reuniting with the Taran Empire, we will soon be able to take an even greater step forward.

"The rumors about Guard fleet movement toward Mysar are false. Elusia stands with Mysar now and into the future. We would not have reached this stage of negotiations with the Empire if we did not believe it would bring us a better future, and we will continue in good faith knowing that our new allies can be trusted with our lives.

"No false rumors will come between us. Elusia and Mysar will soon be reunited with the Taran Empire, and a new era can begin."

Ellen took notes while he spoke. The messaging fit with her needs as perfectly as it would placate Joris' critics.

"Excellent, sir. I'll get this drafted right away."

He nodded absently. "Thank you, Ellen. I'm glad to have you on the team."

That opinion wouldn't last much longer.

"Of course, Mr. President. I'm happy to be of service."

— — —

"Are you sure you want to sit in on this?" Kaen asked Olvera.

She crossed her arms and raised an eyebrow. "Are you

honestly questioning whether the head of base security would want to skip an interrogation with someone suspected of leaking information?"

"I see your point, Major," Kaen conceded. "For the sake of transparency, have you faced security breaches like this before?"

"Never three independent incidents at once. If past events have shown me anything, it's that not all motivations are completely malicious."

"I doubt there's a valid reason for anyone to leak that information."

Olvera gazed at him levelly. "Try to keep an open mind, sir. You have to understand the intentions in order to best understand why the leaks happened and how to prevent them in the future."

The colonel waited, as she looked like she wanted to say more.

"Take, for instance, an incident some years back where a comm tech was recruited by an outside contact to relay classified transcripts."

"To what end?" Kaen questioned, his eyes narrowing.

"Political agenda, like so many things are. The recipient wanted information about the inner workings of the Guard to use as sound bites for their campaign."

"That seems like an awful lot of trouble."

Olvera cracked a smile. "Well, it's actually kind of funny how it went down."

"That doesn't sound like a humorous situation."

"Oh, you'd think that... but it was the transcripts the comm tech got. It's all connected to how she was ultimately caught."

Kaen studied her. "Okay, I'll bite. What were the

transcripts?"

Olvera rubbed her hands together. "As you know, the internal communications system is a catch-all platform for official military orders and any personal business. As a culture, we don't want to place higher value on personal or professional privacy, so it all gets the same level of encryption."

"Right."

"So, this new comm tech didn't seem to realize that the tagging on communications gets stripped away during the encryption process—it's part of the decoding that happens on the receiving end. She came across this message talking about a plan of attack. Five units were set to converge on a target codenamed 'Red 7'. Now, I don't know how familiar you are with Corsica, but the seventh planet in the system is red in color, commonly called 'Roja VII'."

"Ah, all right," Kaen acknowledged.

"Anyway, the comm tech has been watching deployment orders for weeks, waiting for something juicy to come through. When she sees that 'Red 7' is listed as a target—presumably a planned attack against a civilian population—it's the kind of sound bite this politician really needs to perfectly drive home their point. However, all of those dire war plans were really about making sure ol' McGavin had a great birthday party in the commissary."

Kaen sighed.

"It gets better! The comm tech can't just sit back while such an unconscionable, brutal act toward civilians unfolds, so she freaks out. The attack is going to go down any minute, and no one is responding to her messages. She decides to track down the ranking general at the time, Haloway."

"Oh no…"

"Oh *yes*! The general is, naturally, at the very party

discussed in this woefully misinterpreted communication. The comm tech bursts into the mess hall shouting, 'General! I demand you call off the attack on Roja VII!' General Haloway looks back at the tech, understandably confused, and explains that there's no planned attack on a peaceful world in the Empire. Comm tech insists that she's seen the order and soon everyone will know about the Guard's treachery.

"At that very moment, Cindy—who was interning in the general's office at the time—comes in with this layer cake and way more candles than the fire code allows. She tried to duck around the comm tech, but the tech managed to fling her arm at just the right angle to launch the whole flaming tower straight into the air."

"What a waste of perfectly good cake."

Olvera shook her head. "That's the crazy thing! This cake must have gone a good half-meter in the air, but somehow the comm tech caught the bomaxed thing perfectly intact. Once it was safely on the table, the tech got grilled about what she was so upset about. When they realized that the comm tech had been conspiring with an outsider, Colonel Tanaka was ready to initiate court martial proceedings on the spot, but General Haloway was so amused by circumstances surrounding the incident that he decided to grant the comm tech a chance to set things right, given her otherwise exemplary service record."

"Wow," Kaen breathed.

"I wouldn't have believed it if I hadn't been there to see it myself."

"Who was the comm tech?"

Olvera smiled. "Me."

"Seriously...?"

"Disillusioned youth." She shrugged. "I'd like to sit in on the interview and give you my best estimate of whether they'll do it again. Discipline is your purview. Security is mine, and having a leak means I've failed. I need to earn my keep."

"I understand." Kaen nodded. "I have to warn you, though, I don't think we'll have any cake."

"That's a shame, but probably for the best."

Kaen chuckled. "Deanna, you are full of surprises."

The two officers met up with a pair of soldiers—not that Kaen would need any help handling their intended prisoner.

He led the way to the holding cell where the first of their three perpetrators was being detained. Given the seriousness of the violations, Kaen decided it was best to start with the captain, especially since part of his role included consultations with Olvera's security team.

"Captain Ellis," Kaen clasped his hands behind his back as he approached the cell, "we'd like to have a word with you."

"Colonel! What's this about?" The captain ran up to the plexiglass.

"We'll have a private chat." Kaen nodded to the two soldiers, and they opened the cell door.

Ellis turned around and placed his hands behind his back so the armed escorts could cuff him. "There must be some mistake."

"We'll see."

The two soldiers led Ellis to an interrogation room twelve meters down the hall and cuffed him to a bar welded onto the table. When he was secure, the colonel and the chief of security entered.

"I apologize for the restraints, Captain Ellis, but the nature of our accusations requires a degree of caution," Kaen said as he paced on the far side of the table.

Olvera leaned against the wall next to the door with her arms crossed, gaze fixed on the captain.

"Sir, I don't know what you think I—"

"You forwarded a deployment order to the Elusian government, did you not?" Kaen asked.

Ellis took a slow breath. "Yes, I did."

"Care to enlighten us as to why?"

The captain's eyes shifted between Kaen and Olvera. "Those reasons aren't important."

"That isn't for you to decide!" Kaen snarled, slamming his hands on the tabletop. "Who were you working for?"

"Okay, okay!" Ellis shrank back in his chair. "I don't have any name, I swear it. I received a message three years ago while I was on my way home from leave—from a group advocating Elusian unification. I grew up on Elusia, as you've no doubt seen in my file, and I'm sick of the petty arguments between Elusians and the Mysaran Coalition. They asked me to keep an eye on things in the Guard and let them know if there was ever something that might threaten the peace. I've only relayed four pieces of information in those three years. An offensive posture toward Mysar was something I couldn't let slide."

"Captain," Kaen halted his pacing and leaned forward on the table. "You shouldn't have been looking in that folder in the first place."

"With all due respect, Colonel, it's a public folder. As a member of the security team, it's my duty to take a random sampling of documents from across the servers to make sure there are no malicious files."

"That excuse won't cut it," Olvera interjected. "Software takes care of that sampling."

"And I'm the person who makes sure the software is doing its job," Ellis shot back. "Regardless, I didn't hack into a folder where I wasn't supposed to be. You can accuse me of transmitting content outside the Guard, but don't tell me that

I went digging somewhere unauthorized."

"Maybe so," Kaen agreed. "However, I believe you know more about this mystery organization. Tell me."

The captive looked down at his bound hands. "I honestly don't know much more than I've already said. But it might be worth noting what I *don't* know."

Kaen slammed his palms on the table top. "Don't give me that shite, Ellis! You're a disgrace to the uniform, sharing the Guard's secrets—"

Ellis stiffened. "I know my career is probably over, so take the information or leave it. I tried to find the organization, but they're ghosts! As far as I can tell, there *is* no organization doing the things that they've claimed to have done."

"Then why did you keep feeding them information?" Kaen demanded.

"Because the first information I sent was acted upon in a way I agreed with, as were the others. It wasn't until this most recent incident that things seemed... off."

"Deception always bites you in the ass," Kaen grumbled.

"Sir, you're not listening. If this group isn't actually part of the Elusian sphere, then who are they?"

"You tell me, Captain."

"I wish I knew. But I can say that they seem to want peace with the Mysarans, and that sounds good to me."

"Except that you swore your allegiance to the Taran Empire." Kaen stared down his subordinate. "Or have you turned against your oath?"

"My dedication to the Empire will never waver. I'm just not sure that bullying others into joining us is the answer."

"You think we're 'bullying' the Elusians and the Mysarans into rejoining the Empire?"

Ellis shifted in his chair. "This arrangement has left the

people divided. What choice do Elusians now have but to agree to the reunification terms? You've eliminated every other option unless they want to start a civil war."

Kaen perched on the edge of the table. "Captain, you've missed the entire point of the Taran Empire. When we look beyond our individual political boundaries, we become more. By demonstrating that your allegiance is greater to your home nation than to the Empire, you've told us that you don't support that vision of unification.

"And on a final note, the Guard doesn't have anything to do with negotiations. That's the politicians' job. We fill a security role, or have you forgotten that, too?"

"I support the Empire, even if you don't believe me."

"You have your convictions, I'll give you that." Kaen rose from the table. "Unfortunately, those convictions don't align with the integrity demanded of our Guard officers."

Ellis shook his head. "Then I want nothing more to do with this organization."

Kaen glared at the captive. "You turned against *us*! You made a conscious choice to leak classified information. I don't care how you want to justify it—you didn't uphold your duty to the Guard."

Olvera took a step forward toward the table. "You don't believe you've done anything wrong, do you?"

"I did what I had to do."

Kaen shook his head. "Ellis, your service record spoke of loyalty, but I think you were just good at hiding your dishonor. You'll remain in custody until formal charges can be rendered, but rest assured, we won't put you in a position again of having to decide who to give our secrets to."

The captain's shoulders sagged as he looked away from the rage in the colonel's eyes.

Kaen stormed out of the room, followed by Olvera. He walked ten meters down the hall away from the two guards standing to either side of the interrogation room door.

"Think he's being honest?" Olvera asked.

Kaen closed his eyes and took calming breaths. "Tell me your impression."

"I believe he *thinks* he's being honest, at least. But something doesn't feel right to me," she started. "Claiming that he's been feeding information to a phantom group was a bit of a stretch."

"Actually," Kaen countered, "that was probably the truest statement of them all. It's his motivations that don't make sense. Not to sound like a recruiter ad, but people are fiercely loyal to the Guard's mission—pursuit of the greater good. That's why General Haloway forgave your indiscretion; you were trying to help people you thought were being unjustly harmed."

"But Ellis' interests were in service to a specific nation."

"Exactly. People like that don't make it into the Guard in the first place."

"Do you think he was faking it all along?"

Kaen shook his head. "No. Without genuine commitment, a person would never have the motivation to make it through basic training, let alone eleven years of service. I think that chance encounter Ellis mentioned he had while on leave wasn't just a chat. He was directed."

"You don't mean… brainwashing?" Olvera frowned.

"There's precedent for it—you remember how things were during the Priesthood's fall. The TSS gave us the all-clear for the Priesthood's neurotoxin, but I won't rule out any possibility in this investigation, not knowing who's behind it. All I know is that man we spoke to wasn't talking like a Guard officer."

"I guess we need to talk with the others and see if they're acting the same way."

"Yes, we do. I'll defer final judgment on wrongdoing until we know if they've been compromised. These expressed ideals might not be their own."

Olvera's scowl deepened. "If they've been programmed to think and act in certain ways, then who else may not be themselves?"

Kaen released a long breath. "I'm concerned what the answer to that question might be."

CHAPTER 9

KIRA EXITED LEON'S car outside her cottage. "Thanks for seizing that opportunity today. I think I'm so used to being covert that I'm blind to the 'easy way'."

Leon closed the driver's side door and leaned his forearms on the top of the car. "Nothing about this way will be easy, either. Don't kid yourself."

"I'm not. They'll be watching me even closer than you. At least this way, I won't have to make up excuses to be there."

"Given the way that receptionist looked at you, I don't think I would have a hard time explaining to her why I kept stopping by." Kira snapped her mouth shut a moment too late to prevent her foot from entering. *Shite! Did I just say that out loud?*

Leon bust out laughing.

Kira's cheeks burned.

"I hope you're not trying to reduce me just to my looks," Leon said, his voice still filled with mirth.

"That was inappropriate, sorry." She turned away.

"Kira…" He jogged around the car toward her and placed his hand gently on her shoulder. "We've known each other forever. You don't need to explain."

"This isn't a social visit. I should be treating you as a professional."

"Official Guard business or not, we're still old friends. I'm glad we can still joke around."

She softened. "You're right. Present circumstances aside, you're Lee."

"Oh, stars, no one's called me that in years!" Leon exclaimed through a chuckle. "I always hated that nickname."

"But you let me get away with using it, anyway."

"Because I knew if I tried to get you to stop, you'd just turn it into sport. It was easier to find it endearing." He slid his hand down her arm, and his fingers brushed against hers.

Their eyes met.

Kira drew a deep breath and stepped back toward her cottage. "I shouldn't keep you from your evening. I might wander over to that gym you told me about."

"Nonsense. Have dinner with me. I'll take you to the gym tomorrow."

"Leon…"

"I insist. Besides, pretty sure those cupboards are completely bare. If you want to eat—and I know how you like your dinners—you'll need to subsist off those of us who actually live here." He cocked his head. "Whaddya say?"

"All right, fine," Kira yielded. *Stars, I'm entirely too motivated by food.* Not that the company was a deterrent…

"Wow, that didn't take much."

"Admittedly, you had me at 'eat'."

He shook his head and laughed. "Kira, you've hardly changed a bit."

"That's Captain Bit," she jested. "Don't forget that I can disarm you fifty different ways in two seconds flat. A fact I intend to demonstrate at the gym later."

"…You say to the person who you could control with a bat of your eyelashes when we were sixteen."

"Granted, that 'you' wasn't *you* specifically."

"Relax, I'm just giving you a hard time."

Kira smiled. "What's on the menu for tonight?"

"I've been slow-roasting a pork tenderloin for the last eighteen hours, and I gathered greens from my garden. I just have to throw a loaf of bread in the oven, which was crafted from a sourdough starter passed down in my family for five generations."

Kira's mouth dropped open. "You shouldn't have…"

"Oh, good! Because we're just having noodle packets." He grinned. "Stars, Kira, I have a doctorate in genetics and regularly work eleven-hour days in an underground lab. You won't find a master chef over here."

Smooth. She sighed. "You know, noodles sound just fine."

— — —

Kira awoke the following morning with a grin after the evening with Leon. It had been years since she'd had a proper night of relaxation, and she could think of few people who offered better company. Though there were moments of flirtation, Leon was a perfect gentleman, as always. Kira knew all too well just how hard that was to find.

Still, the mission came first. After the business with MTech was straightened out, she could revisit the past.

A knock sounded on Kira's front door while she was blow-drying her hair. "Coming!"

She finished up and ran for the door in the low heels she'd paired with slacks and a long-sleeve blouse. *Leon isn't supposed to be here for another five minutes!*

Except it wasn't Leon at the door.

"Mom, Dad? How did you—"

"Kira!" her mother exclaimed. "Why didn't you tell us you were coming back to visit?"

Yet another complication I don't need. "This isn't a vacation."

"I don't care why you're here," her father said. "We haven't seen you for ages. We've missed you."

Kira deflated. "Leon told you I was here, didn't he?"

"We're still good friends with his parents. They mentioned it to us," her mother confirmed.

Way to keep things undercover, Leon! Kira took a step back into the living room and left the door open for her parents to enter. There was no way they would leave without getting some semblance of an explanation. "I know I should call more often. The Guard keeps me busy."

Her father closed the front door behind him. "Such a waste of your gifts."

Oh, here we go. Kira's eyes narrowed. "No, Dad, a waste would have been staying here and playing games with tourists. I am out there helping the rest of the galaxy."

"Come on, Harold, arguing won't get us anywhere," Kira's mother placed a hand on her husband's arm.

"Don't pretend you haven't thought the same things, Ruth."

Is it any wonder I don't call often? Kira took a calming breath. "I not sure what Leon's parents may have told you, but I don't have time to socialize right now."

"You can't take a few minutes for your parents?" Harold

asked.

Kira held in a groan. "I need a few days to get my head in the right place."

"We didn't mean to barge in on you," her mother said.

"I didn't mean it like that."

In recent years, it seemed like any of Kira's conversations with her parents quickly turned into a guilt trip or misunderstanding in one way or another. They'd had hopes for her to follow in her grandmother's footsteps and become a Reader in their local community, but Kira's military aspirations had derailed their plans for her. Even after a numerous attempts to explain, they'd never understood her desire to put her life at risk to help strangers—their perspective was too focused on their small, peaceful world in a city where hotel over-booking was the biggest concern.

Kira centered herself. "Look, you caught me by surprise. Let's start over."

Her mother smiled. "Good idea. Are soldiers allowed to give hugs?" She held out her arms.

A smile broke through on Kira's face. "Of course." She stepped forward and embraced her mother.

Ruth rocked Kira back and forth. "Whatever brought you back here, I'm glad to see you doing well." She pulled back from the hug and brushed her fingers along Kira's short hair at her temple.

"No long braids in the Guard," Kira replied to the unspoken question.

Her mother nodded and silently admired her.

"All right, now. Don't keep her all to yourself." Harold wrapped Kira in a bear hug.

"It's good to see you too, Dad," she mumbled into his shoulder. He released her.

"I'm sorry I haven't stayed in touch," Kira continued. "So much of what I'm working on is classified."

"You're okay. That's the important thing," Ruth said as she hesitantly took a step back toward the door. "We should let you finish getting settled in. Maybe we can have lunch later to catch up?"

"I'd love to, but—"

"Oh, sorry to interrupt."

Kira turned to see Leon standing in the doorway. "We have to get over to the MTech lab," Kira finished her statement. "I'm sorry, this just isn't a good time. I should be less distracted in a few days."

Harold frowned. "What are you doing over there with MTech?"

"Working on a special project," Kira replied.

Her parents frowned.

"They're very impressed with her," Leon chimed in on her behalf. He held up a white paper bag. "I got you a scone for the road."

Bringing me fresh pastries? That almost made up for tipping off her parents. "Thanks."

She took one of each of her parents' hands. "I need to take care of this business, but once I'm done, we can spend some time together. I promise."

Ruth pulled her in for another hug. "I hope you mean that."

"I do. This isn't like that time."

She parted ways from her parents, feeling simultaneously relieved that the overdue reunion was out of the way and also nervous for how she'd answer their inevitable questions about what she'd been up to for the last decade. There was no easy way to explain that she'd been trained as a killer and had been involved in pivotal events that had impacted thousands of lives. Even if they professed to be proud of her—which she wasn't sure they would—she knew their perception of their little girl would be forever changed.

They said their goodbyes, and her parents climbed into their vehicle, waving while they backed out.

Once the car was down the driveway, Kira sighed and fixed Leon with dagger eyes. "You shouldn't have told anyone I was here."

"Don't pull that 'undercover op' shite, Kira. Your cover *is* you returning home. It'd be suspicious if you didn't see your parents while you were back here supposedly reconnecting with your roots. I put the word out there because I knew you wouldn't do it yourself."

Kira huffed. "Give me that scone, Puppetmaster."

He chuckled and handed over the bag. "Don't worry, I have no intention of controlling your life or pretending I know what's best for you. I just know MTech and how they think. That's why I'm here to help."

"Next time, check with me first."

"Would you have agreed?" he asked.

"Probably not."

Leon raised an eyebrow.

"All right, fine. Maybe this was a helpful nudge in the right direction, one friend to another."

"Family can be challenging. I'll be the first to admit it."

"You didn't bail on your folks like I did."

He hesitated. "I think all of us would have liked a little more warning, not going to lie."

"I learned my lesson, believe me." Kira looked him over. His gaze met hers for a moment, but she quickly refocused on the task at hand. "Anyway, thanks for helping me maintain my cover. Most of my recent missions have involved blowing things up with tac teams and plasma rifles, so I'm still remembering how to do this whole subtle infiltration thing."

"Remember faster, because we have to get to the lab."

She scowled playfully. "What do you take me for?"

"Yes, your majesty, I know you're a pro. Come on, you can eat in the car."

Kira grinned. "Good, because I was going to anyway."

She had devoured the scone by the time the car had made it out of the housing complex to the main road. While she licked the orange frosting from her fingers, she gazed out the window at the surrounding hills and the wispy clouds drifting through the sky.

Sky. It had been years since she'd spent any appreciable time on a planet. Space had become her home. Yet, being back on Valta and feeling real gravity underfoot, breathing fresh air, she realized that she did miss being planetside. Perhaps future assignments would afford more time on the ground.

They arrived at the MTech parking lot and then got out and walked the short path to the facility's entrance.

Once inside, Kira approached the reception desk. "Good morning."

"Hello, Kira," Martha greeted. "I have your visitor badge for you." She handed it over the counter. "I'll let Dr. Waylon know you're here."

"No need to bother her," Leon said. "I can get Kira oriented to whatever assignment Dr. Waylon wanted her to work on."

"I was given specific instructions." Martha made entries on the desktop in front of her. "You can get to your duties, Dr. Calleti. I'll keep Kira company while she waits."

Kira gave Leon a nod to let him know it was all right.

He acquiesced. "Very well. Maybe I'll see you at lunch?"

"I'll let you know," Kira said. "If not, dinner."

He smiled. "Have a good day." He headed for the security arch into A Wing.

"Any more details involved with the orders Dr. Waylon left?" Kira asked the receptionist.

"No, but your badge now has access to C Wing."

"What's in there?" Kira already had a rough idea based on Leon's orientation, but she was curious how Martha would reply.

"It's some of our most exciting technology. You're in for a treat."

"Looking forward to it."

When Martha didn't say anything more, Kira began strolling around the lobby, making note of the security details and points for entry or emergency egress. While sleek and architecturally stunning, the place was built like a fortress—but every fortress had its vulnerabilities.

"Enjoying the view?" Monica said from behind Kira.

She turned to greet her. "I was admiring those pendant lights. Were they made by our local glass craftsmen at Trileo Studio?"

"Good eye. They were," Monica confirmed. "We tried to bring as much local flavor to the facility as possible. MTech is grateful to have been welcomed to Valta with such open arms."

Like anyone had a choice, I'm sure. Kira smiled. "That's great to see. So, what did you want to meet with me about?"

"Come. We'll talk in private."

Monica led her to the security arch on the left. In contrast to A Wing's door-lined corridors, this wing entrance was a featureless hallway that terminated in an elevator door.

"Your secret lair?" Kira asked.

"Hardly." Monica pressed the call button. "Due to the

nature of the research in this division, we constructed the lab four stories underground to minimize external interference."

The logic was sound, but the hairs on the back of Kira's neck stood up when the elevator door opened. *If I don't go with her now, I'm out for good.* She steeled her nerves and stepped into the elevator car.

The control panel consisted of a single button, marked 'Sublevel 4'.

They rode down the four stories in silence. When the doors opened, the temperature was a couple of degrees cooler than on the surface, even though Kira detected the telltale signs of environmental controls.

"I have a lab set aside for us to chat in," Monica said as she stepped into the corridor.

The hallway more closely resembled A Wing, but Kira was still on edge. She didn't like being in a place with only one way out.

"Dr. Waylon—er, Monica—may I ask why you've taken an interest in me rather than any of the other Readers on Valta? I'm hardly the only telepath around here."

"Oh, I have spoken with others. I'm curious to see how an extended time away from Valta has impacted your abilities."

A slight pitch in her tone gave her away. *She's lying.*

Kira had been given complete authority to use any means necessary for investigation, so she may as well take advantage of that freedom. She prepared for an assessment of Monica's inner thoughts.

Invading someone's mind turned her stomach, especially for someone who hadn't actually done anything to wrong her—yet. Still, the MTech lab was up to something, and there wouldn't be an easier way to find out what that was other than to read the lab director's thoughts.

Kira waited for the right moment when she was able to make eye contact for long enough to initiate a telepathic link with Monica's mind. However, Kira's probe met only a blank mental wall.

The fok? She tried to push through, but the barrier was impenetrable, even for her advanced skills.

"That's not polite," Monica said without breaking stride.

"Oh, shite." The words slipped out before Kira could stop herself.

Only one group aside from the Readers on Valta were capable of such thorough mental blocks, due to their own telepathic abilities. But that meant Monica had trained as a TSS Agent, and she may also possess telekinetic abilities.

"You're…" Kira began.

"Yes, I spent a year training as a TSS Agent before I was enlightened about their ass-backward ways," Monica completed. "You shouldn't be so surprised, knowing firsthand what it's like to have the military use you for your special abilities."

Kira's pulse spiked. She tried to settle it, knowing the telepath would be able to pick up on the slightest changes to her demeanor. *Shite! Did I tip her off to my mission during our last meeting?* She couldn't remember if she'd tensed or hesitated while responding to any questions. "You've read my file."

"Of course I have. Why do you think I was so eager to chat with you? You are quite a fascinating individual, Kira Elsar."

"My abilities aren't like those who train with the TSS," Kira said after a pause.

"Yes, you are quite a curious case." Monica studied her. "Telepathy but none of the other traits that are typically associated with the Gifted bloodlines."

"Makes us Valtan telepaths kinda boring compared to a telekinetic like you."

Monica smiled slightly. "I've never liked that name, since the abilities are more than just object levitation and what one typically thinks of as 'telekinesis'. I much prefer the 'Gifted' label rather than calling us 'TK'."

Kira had heard that some Gifted could perform extraordinary feats beyond levitation—electromagnetic manipulation, focusing their power through objects, ultra-fast movements through spatial distortions. She had no interest in finding out the extent of Monica's abilities firsthand.

"What do you expect to learn from me that you don't already know from your own experience?" Kira asked.

A slight smile touched Monica's lips. "I'm certain you've seen the recent news reports about the Priesthood's genetic experimentations on Tararia—how their interventions led to the Generation Cycle, yes?"

Kira nodded. The information she'd seen had been sensationalized by the media, but there must have been enough truth in it for the High Dynasties to have successfully removed the Priesthood from power. According to the recent information leaks, telepathic and telekinetic abilities used to be much more common, except clandestine genetic modifications gone wrong had permanently altered the general population. Learning that, it was no surprise Kira's ancestors had chosen to flee the central worlds.

"Well, the powers that be have been looking for a genetic patch," Monica continued. "Since the origins of Valta's telepathic skills appear to be distinct from standard Taran gifts, learning more about the expression of your abilities might yield insights about how to correct other genetic anomalies."

"What *kind* of study?" Kira pressed.

"I'd like to take a look inside your brain."

Kira tensed. She was down four stories with no way to get in touch with anyone. Her hands curled into fists, ready to fight her way out if she needed to.

"Are you all right?" Monica asked, pausing in the middle of the hall.

"What are you going to do to me?" Kira demanded.

Monica stared at her for five seconds then broke into a musical laugh. "What, do you think I brought you down here to lock you up like a lab animal?" She placed a hand on Kira's shoulder and looked her in the eyes. "Kira, I just want to learn more about the nature of your abilities—a non-invasive examination. You needn't worry."

The words were genuine, as far as Kira could tell, but it was all way too suspicious. This woman was hiding something, and Kira could tell that she personally somehow fit into a larger plan. However, there was no way that she could take on a combatant with telekinetic abilities single-handedly. She needed to play along.

"Sorry, I just get a bit claustrophobic underground."

Monica raised one of her shapely eyebrows. "Even after all your time in space?"

"We have viewports. It's a weird psychological quirk, what can I say?"

"One of the great things that makes us special." The doctor smiled.

Kira held out her hand. "Lead the way."

They traversed another fifteen meters of hall and then turned to the left. Monica opened the second door on the right, revealing a stark white five-by-five meter room with a table and two chairs in the center and a computer panel along the back wall.

"Have a seat." Monica walked to the computer and began navigating through a menu.

Kira selected the chair with the better view of the door. "You're not big on color around here."

"The white brings some brightness to the space, though, don't you think?"

"I suppose."

Monica stopped her entries on the touchscreen and turned to face Kira. "Have I offended you in some way by inviting you here?"

All right, time to try a straight approach. Kira shrugged. "I know you're busy and must have a lot of other, better things to do than talk with some Guard officer visiting Valta on leave. I'm curious what you're working on that would make me a priority."

The director glided toward the table and took the seat across from Kira. "MTech selected Valta for our research because of the unique properties of this planet. People have dedicated decades of their lives to cracking its secrets, but no one has been successful. I want to do what no one else has done.

"You are a unique case among your people—no other Reader has resided offworld. We know Valtan babies born away from this planet don't inherit their parents' abilities, so why are you able to live elsewhere and retain them? As a scientist, that's one of the most intriguing case studies I've ever come across."

Kira had to admit that she had always been curious about that phenomenon herself. While she didn't like the idea of being scrutinized in a lab, if Monica could offer some answers while Kira conducted her own investigation, she'd love to know.

"How did you get involved in genetics research?" Kira

asked.

Monica rose from the table and resumed her entries on the computer. "I began as a nanoscientist, actually. I was always fascinated by the interplay between technology and biology."

That certainly sounds like the mission brief from Kaen. If MTech has a strain of nanites for the Robus, this woman is behind it. She leaned back in her chair. "What have you learned?"

"That there's a lot we don't know about our universe."

"Stars, yeah. But, surely, you've picked up some interesting knowledge along the way."

"Oh, of course." Monica flashed a smile. "It's all very technical, though. I won't bore you."

Pressing any more would sound suspicious, so Kira switched gears. "Has your research into Valta extended beyond the Readers?"

"Yes, very much so. I'm interested in the unique telepathic bonds shared across this world," Monica replied. "If we can understand what about Valta results in such sensitivities, then we can, by extension, get that much closer to transferring those properties into other vehicles—such as nanites."

"That'd probably be the discovery of the century—if not the millennia."

"Perhaps now you understand why I'll go down any research path available to crack that code. I hope you'll lend a hand."

The mission aside, Kira had to admit that it was a fascinating concept. "I'll do what I can."

"Thank you, Kira." Monica walked to a cabinet on the right wall and pulled out a cylindrical contraption and a transparent box filled with what appeared to be medical electrodes.

"This equipment is designed to measure the unique

electromagnetic energy associated with telepathic and telekinetic abilities. I'd like to expose you to some stimuli and test your response," the doctor explained. She placed the cylinder on the table. "Would that be all right?"

I'm committed to the course now. "Of course, go right ahead."

Kira sat rigidly while Monica affixed the electrodes around her head, on the upper part of her chest, and to her wrists.

"Excellent. We'll begin in a moment." Monica disconnected one of the monitors on the computer to use as a tablet.

Taking a deep breath, Kira nodded. She trusted in her own mental blocks and would only reveal whatever would advance her toward her desired ends with Monica.

The lights dimmed to half-brightness when Monica slid her hand along the edge of the tablet screen. A holographic representation of Tribeca appeared above the cylinder.

"Do you recognize this location?" Monica asked.

"Yes, of course. It's this city."

"And what is your connection to this place?"

"It was my home. I grew up here."

"And now?"

Kira thought for a second. "It's still the place where I spent my childhood, but it's no longer my home."

"How do you feel looking at this image?"

"Nostalgic, I guess."

Monica tilted her head. "Why is that?"

"Answers were a lot clearer when I was young."

The doctor made a note on her tablet. "Physically, how does it feel to be back here?"

Ah, now we're getting down to it. Kira folded her hands on the tabletop. "It was energizing when I stepped off the shuttle, if that's what you mean."

"Can you recall how it compared to when you lived here?"

Honestly, Kira couldn't. It had been so long since Valta was her home, now she was only a few steps removed from being a tourist herself. "This place has been a part of me since I was conceived. Leaving didn't change that, but I feel... fuller here than I do anywhere else."

Monica nodded and set down her tablet. "With many subjects, I can easily talk around my real questions. That's not the case with you."

Kira smiled. "It is my job, after all. My guess is that you're trying to gauge how my telepathic link changes based on where I am?"

"Yes, and specifically, Valta as a power source, of sorts."

"When it comes to people developing telepathy, I've always thought of Valta as more of a nursery than a creator," Kira replied. "Based on my own experience and stories I've heard from others, it seems like this place can take a seed of potential and let it flower. Someone with no genetic potential won't spontaneously develop abilities here and, assuming those abilities are hereditary, their children won't, either. But for those who do have the genetic potential, it can be unlocked here."

The MTech scientist nodded.

"Now," Kira continued, "given that abilities take a generation or two to show up, there must be something here that saturates a person over time. Water, soil, the electromagnetic field—I have no idea what. Or maybe it's not any one thing, but rather a unique confluence of features."

It was more than Kira had intended to say on the subject, but she was genuinely curious to get the scientist's take on her homeworld.

"That's a very astute observation, Kira. I like that nursery analogy." Monica turned off the holoprojector and raised the light level. "What I find most interesting, though, is how your brain responded when shown a picture of Tribeca. There was increased activity in the cerebral structures my research has shown are most connected to telepathic potential."

Kira's heart leaped. "Really?"

The doctor inclined her head. "This suggests to me that, for those who were 'nurtured' here, there is an enduring connection."

"I guess so..." *So much for being a straightforward recon assignment! Now I want her research to continue.* Kira suppressed the thought.

"If you don't mind, I'd like to set you up in a lab with more sensitive equipment while you run through some telepathic exercises. I'm curious how much energy you draw and how that compares to others I've interviewed."

"Yeah, sure," Kira agreed, though she wasn't crazy about being down in the underground lair longer than necessary.

"I prepped a setup, just in case. I'm pleased you were able to so quickly confirm my suspicions."

That goes both ways, Doctor, Kira thought as she rose from the table and followed Monica into the hall.

The second exam room was two doors down on the left. This one was equipped with a single padded chair and a table at the center of the three-meter square room, completed with acoustic tiles. On the table sat a gerbil in a glass atrium.

"Um..." Kira's gaze shifted between the rodent and Monica. "What...?"

"Ah, yes." Monica beckoned for Kira to take the chair facing the gerbil. "This room is outfitted with advanced monitoring equipment that will supplement the readings gathered through your electrodes. We found it to be an invasion of privacy to have telepaths read other humans, so a rodent serves as a stand-in."

Kira plopped into the chair. "I hate to be a poor sport here, but I can't mind-read a gerbil."

"It's not so much reading a mind, as attempting to."

"So… you want me to bore into the soul of a creature with the brain the size of a pea?" She let the sarcasm really shine through with her tone.

Monica smiled, stepping to the door. "It'll only take an hour or so to gather the necessary readings."

Kira stared into the gerbil's black eyes. It cooed at her.

She sighed. *Fok my life.*

CHAPTER 10

KAEN LEANED BACK in his chair across the interrogation table from the second suspect.

The young lieutenant's gaze was darting around the room, presumably trying to spot monitoring equipment.

Does she think she can break out, or does she want to work a deal under the table without others knowing? Kaen glanced back at Olvera and she shrugged.

"I asked you a question, Lieutenant," Kaen reiterated.

"Yes, I transmitted that file outside of the Guard secure servers," Lieutenant Morgan replied at last.

Kaen leaned against the table. "Why?"

Morgan didn't flinch.

Young people could be so frustratingly stubborn. "Why?" he snarled inching closer to her.

She shook her head and looked away. "If you're going to court martial or execute me or whatever, just get it over with."

Kaen backed away and took a softer approach. "Morgan, I don't want this to end badly for you. If you had a valid reason for violating those orders, it may change the punishment."

"We all make mistakes," Olvera offered.

"Oh, this wasn't a mistake." Morgan scoffed. "I knew *exactly* what I was doing."

"You're not leaving this room until you provide some indication about the *why*," Kaen stated. "If you don't cooperate, we'll bring in an interrogator who's sure to get results."

That got her attention. "It was about my parents. They've… had a tough go of it. I joined the Guard to get out of that life, and I send money when I can. But it's not enough."

The notion that some citizens didn't have the resources they needed to lead a comfortable life was not unknown to him, but conditions had improved considerably since the recent leadership changes on Tararia. There must have been extenuating circumstances for her family to still be facing considerable hardships, assuming her statements were true. "So, you were… selling this information?" Kaen prompted.

"No. Well, not exactly. They said that they'd help my parents if I just fed little bits of information here and there. Nothing too classified, just some mission briefs. They said it was a 'heads up' to give them a chance to take action, if ever it was needed."

"And who's 'they'?"

"Some government official with the Mysaran Coalition."

Kaen groaned inwardly. *That confirms the suspicion that these leaks are independent. First the Elusians, now the Mysarans…* "Do you have a name?"

"They went by Nox."

Kaen glanced back at Olvera.

"If you'll excuse me," the security chief said and left the room.

"So, this Nox, can you tell me any more about him… or her?"

"Their voice was distorted the one time we spoke. The other communications were all text."

"How did you meet?"

"Three years ago at a spaceport. It was during some R&R after a field training op," Morgan replied.

Same timeframe as the captain, Kaen mused. "Is that when you spoke?"

"No." She crossed her arms. "It's strange. I can't remember exactly how the meeting happened. All I know for sure is I got a note that directed me to a bar, and there was a package waiting for me. I looked over the offer; it explained what I'd have to do and that I'd never have to worry about my parents again. It was a pretty dire situation at the time, so I couldn't refuse."

"Your parents are doing better now?"

"It's not glamorous, but they're way better off than they were."

Thanks to Nox, or did the mysterious benefactor simply have their hand on the pulse of Taran politics, anticipating this turnaround? Kaen nodded and placed a hand on his chin. "Have your parents ever spoken about their benefactor?"

"No, there's never been any direct contact. I tried tracing some of the supply shipments sent to their home, but it all led to ghosts."

Perhaps there is *someone working behind the scenes. If it's a government official, they might have the means to mask the origin. But is there a common thread connecting the leaks?* Part of Kaen was excited for the investigative challenge, but the implications were concerning, to say the least. Either two people had coincidentally similar experiences at the same time, or there was a third party at play to maneuver two governments against each other. Two incidents didn't constitute a pattern—he'd still have to speak with the third suspect and see if that filled in any of the missing pieces.

"Lieutenant, I understand your desire to help your parents, but this is a serious offense."

She bristled. "I don't regret it. I'd do it again."

"Integrity and honor above all." Kaen rose from the table. "I'll contemplate whether you get a court martial or not."

"Just leave my parents out of it."

"The Guard is a humanitarian organization. We'd never do anything to harm civilians." He exited and turned her over to the guards waiting outside the door.

Olvera was hurrying back down the hall, tablet in hand. "Get anything else?"

"No," he replied. "Shame. I hate to see a career thrown away like that."

"She made her choice."

"That part about not remembering the meeting…"

The security chief nodded. "It did sound similar to the circumstances of Captain Ellis' recruitment."

"I agree, and the timing is close."

"Well," Olvera sighed, "if there is someone in the Mysaran government who's connected to all this, their real name isn't 'Nox'."

"I figured as much." Kaen crossed his arms. "We could request detailed receipt records to see where the file went within their system."

"In this political climate? Acting suspicious and showing a lack of trust might not go over so well."

Kaen frowned. "I'm beginning to wonder if that was the whole point of this."

Olvera's face paled. "That is the easiest explanation."

"Except the question remains, who'd want this deal to fall apart?"

—   —   —

By the end of the hour with her new rodent friend—which she'd named Mr. Fuzzers—Kira had developed an insatiable craving for carrots.

Fortunately, Monica informed Kira that she was free to go, if she wished, while Monica's team analyzed the test results. Thoughts of fresh salad from her favorite café in Tribeca had Kira salivating, but she couldn't take the rest of the day off from the mission. Hopefully MTech's cafeteria had a good selection of veggies.

"I don't suppose I could come back tomorrow to go over the test results with you?" Kira asked, easing into her real question.

"Of course. This is as much to educate you about yourself as it is for me to learn about the nature of your abilities."

"Speaking of that, I've always been curious about the genetics side. Might I be able to spend some time in the lab with Leon Calleti?" Kira made a point to keep her breathing and heart rate calm and level while she asked. She hoped that any tells would be interpreted as a crush rather than her planned deception.

"Genetic analysis? With your military background, I'd think you'd be more interested in biotech—our rapid healing aids, or muscle augmentation."

Kira flashed a disarming smile. "Well, yes. But I get so much of that in the course of my day-to-day life that it's so... impersonal. Looking into genetics is something I'd be doing for *me*. Plus," she lowered her voice, "I wouldn't mind a little extra time with him, if you know what I mean."

The doctor chuckled. "I still remember what it was like to be young. I see no harm in you shadowing him." Her gaze lingered on Kira just a moment too long.

She definitely knows I'm up to something. Nothing Kira could do about it now. "Great. Are we done here?"

"Yes." Monica showed her to the door. "I'll have an escort bring you to Dr. Calleti."

"Thanks, I appreciate it." Kira followed her into the hall.

The doctor stopped after two paces and turned back toward Kira. "A word to the wise: don't abuse this generosity, Kira. You don't want to get on my bad side."

"I'd never think of it."

— — —

President Joris swiped his hand across his desk to minimize the news reports. Press statement or not, rumors were still floating around that the Guard had planned to attack a civilian resistance group on Mysar until some hero had uncovered their sneaky plan. He hated how truths became twisted so easily.

With word of the Tararian Guard's involvement, groups previously in support of rejoining the Empire were now questioning that union, citing this incident as a reason to distrust the Empire rather than reunite with their estranged Taran brethren. Others saw the display for what it was and were even more enthusiastic about joining the Taran Empire so they could close the divide for good.

Joris groaned. Being president at the center of the madness was challenging. No matter what he did, he was going to piss off someone. However, if he didn't take action, he risked his people being on one side of a civil war that had no basis in reality.

"Send up Ellen," Joris told Nico, his assistant. He needed to make a formal statement. Not just a press release this time, but a speech.

Ellen arrived three minutes later carrying her customary tablet. "Yes, Mr. President?"

"It's time we have a heart-to-heart with our citizens."

She tilted her head questioningly.

Joris clasped his hands behind his back and began pacing. "We've lived in a state of transition for the past three hundred years. Elusians and Mysarans differ only in our name, yet we continue to provide reasons for disagreement. That divide will tear us apart and destroy our greatest chance for an elevated future unless we come together and commit to a new approach.

"Officially rejoining the Taran Empire won't change who we are—it will afford us the necessary stability and resources to be our best selves. Culture will flourish, and we'll finally be able to set aside the petty disagreements that have plagued our people for the past three centuries. For this reason, I move for immediate ratification of Elusian Alliance's reunification agreement with the Taran Empire and move for the Mysaran Coalition to do likewise."

His press secretary's mouth dropped open. "Sir, that's…"

"You're the wordsmith, Ellen. I'm sure you can come up with a way to soften the blow. But that's the message."

She took a shaky breath. "How do you want this delivered?"

"I'll say it myself. Have a speech draft on my desk by the end of the day. We'll make the announcement at 07:00."

Ellen gave a reluctant nod. "Yes, sir."

Joris watched her leave and then walked up to his window to gaze out over the city. He had no way of knowing how the speech would be received, but he was certain he was about to make history.

— — —

Kira knocked on the outer glass wall of Leon's office. "Hey. Look who you couldn't get rid of."

Her friend glanced up from his work in surprise. "How'd you get over here?"

She shrugged. "I convinced Monica to let me shadow you." She had more to say, but it couldn't be said aloud where others might be listening in.

Gazing into Leon's eyes, she formed a direct telepathic link. *"Pretty sure Monica's going to have security watching me like hawks, so I need you to run interference for me,"* she told him.

He got a look on his face that only an old friend who knew her too well could, already anticipating a crazy plan. He formed a response in his mind, *"What do you have in mind?"*

"Just a little poking around. Nothing too invasive."

He sighed. "What have you seen so far?" he asked aloud.

Kira leaned against the edge of his desk and grabbed a small metal planet model, one of the few personal items on the obsessively tidy desktop. She tossed it back and forth between her hands. "I got to spend the last hour in C Wing communing with a gerbil."

Leon's face scrunched up. "Wait, what?"

"You really don't want to know."

He took the metal planet from her and set it back in its holder, straightening the base to square alignment. He resumed eye contact with her to continue their telepathic conversation. *"Okay, so C Wing. You've already been somewhere I've never had access to. I doubt hanging out here with me is going to get you anywhere."*

"Yeah, but I didn't have a computer down there."

"Kira, you cannot *use my computer to hack into the MTech system,"* Leon said in a terse mental tone.

"When you agreed to be liaison for this mission, you committed to help me out with anything I needed to uncover the target information. Right now, that's use of your computer."

"You're going to get me fired—or worse."

"The very fact that you're worried about an 'or worse' is precisely why we have to do this." She paused. *"But what makes you say that? You didn't give any indication of danger before."*

"I…" He focused on his computer monitor. *"It's probably nothing, but I overheard someone in the break room this morning mention that one of their acquaintances from the employee housing community wasn't around the last two mornings. They normally commuted together."*

"Where'd this person work?"

"That's the only reason I'm mentioning it now. I guess it was some sort of 'special assignment' connected to B Wing in some way."

Kira kicked back in her chair, pretending to wait while Leon looked something up. *"Is that suspicious somehow?"*

"Not unto itself, no. But when I looked him up, Tim Masters, there was no employee record."

"So, either he's been ghosted, he's attached to some secret division, or both."

Leon wilted in his chair. *"You've got it."*

Kira got a devious glint in her eyes. "Hey, I think there's

some really involved genetic model you need to show me on your computer. Maybe teach me how the software is used? Might take some hands-on learning on my part."

"Yeah, I'm happy to give you a demonstration," Leon replied aloud, then added in his mind, *"Shite, Kira, you better help me find a new job when this is over."*

"I'm sure we can work something out." She shooed him from his chair and sat down.

Leon grabbed the visitor chair and pulled it up next to her. "Here, let me pull up an example file for us to walk through." He leaned over and brought up a menu with some genetic sequences and displayed one on the main monitor, which was visible from outside the office. He then cleared part of the interactive desktop to give her a covert place for her hacking work.

"I doubt I'll get very far," she muttered. *"I'll need a passcode to get into anything secure without drawing attention."*

He caught her gaze. *"Are you suggesting doing a Reading of someone?"*

"If I have to. Unfortunately, Monica's the only person I'm certain would have such a passcode, but she's impossible to read."

Leon's brow wrinkled with confusion.

"Oh yeah, by the way, Monica is Gifted—like, she quit TSS telekinesis training."

"What?!" He then continued telepathically, *"Like, an actual...?"*

"Yeah, she must wear contacts to hide the bioluminescent glow. Would have been an Agent if she didn't have such a diabolical streak."

"How do you know she has abilities?" Leon asked, his eyes wide with wonder.

She smiled over her shoulder at him. *"How do you think?"*

"*Shite, Kira. You tried to read her mind? She's probably expecting you to do exactly what you're doing!*"

"*Which is why we have to move quickly. Until she tips her hand, I'm staying the course. I don't have another choice.*"

Leon released a long breath and ran his fingers through his light brown hair.

"Relax," she told him. "Just show me this genetic model of yours."

Kira tuned out Leon's half-hearted explanation of the model while she returned her attention to tunneling through the MTech computer system. Eventually, she reached a quartered off section of the network. "My, my. What have we here?"

"That's a lot of data," Leon commented out loud before he caught himself. "*Must be some serious models, or videos—something—to be hogging that much space.*"

"*Like a whole secret division.*" Kira gnawed on her lip. "*I need to find out where it is, physically.*"

"Kira…"

"*Stop. Be supportive or make no comment.*"

He nodded.

"*Now, when do people normally head home for the day?*"

"Around 18:00 most days. Why?"

"*Because once most people head out, the cleaning crew steps in. And if anyone knows about secret doors in the facility, it's the people operating in the background.*"

"*Even if you find a door, how do you expect to get in?*"

"We find someone with the right access." She smiled. "You really know your stuff with these genetic models.

"Thanks." Leon sighed. "*I never should have agreed to this.*"

"*No take-backsies.*" Kira patted his arm. "*We'll go on an expedition after lunch. Maybe we can catch one of the early cleaning crew."*

"For the record, I do not endorse this plan."

Despite his grumblings, Leon proved to be a good sport for the rest of the morning while Kira counted down the minutes to their lunch break. Her desire for a salad had continued to intensify. At last, he escorted her to the cafeteria, which she'd seen briefly during her tour the prior afternoon.

The room was filled with people from across the A Division. What Leon didn't need to know was that Kira had no intention of tracking down a single individual to give her a lead. If there were people around that wing who knew something relevant, there was a good chance they'd pass through the lunch hub at some point in the next half hour, and she'd get all of their stories.

"Forgive me if I'm not too talkative," Kira said while they got in line. "I'm ravenous. That test this morning really did a number on me."

"Sure, don't worry about it," Leon replied.

Kira cleared her mind and began reaching out to those around her whenever she was able to make brief eye contact, sensing for any indication about their position or access. Since they had just left their stations, current work assignments were at the forefront of their thoughts, making her task far easier than it would have been at any other time.

Most people were low-level techs, but there was the occasional manager. Kira dismissed the first forty people in a matter of thirty seconds, then moved onto the next wave. By the time she was up to the front of the buffet line, she'd vetted close to two hundred people and had encountered no one promising.

Feeling disheartened, she prepared a salad with extra carrots and radishes before finding a seat along the side wall with Leon. She kept her mental scan running in the background while she kept an eye on the room.

"I don't recall you being much of a salad person," Leon commented when they were settled at the table.

"I'm normally not. It was that foking gerbil…"

He almost spit out his first bite of sandwich.

"Yeah, laugh all you want." She stabbed into a piece of carrot and bit off a chunk. *Stars, that's satisfying.*

Kira was trying to think up another witty retort when someone's thoughts caught her attention.

She zeroed in on a man just entering the cafeteria. He wore a white lab coat, like half the other employees, and had a brisk gait that was offset by a twitchiness in his hands. After a brief moment of eye contact with Kira, the man kept his gaze straight ahead until he reached the queue line.

"Whatcha up to?" Leon asked.

"Shh, nothing." Kira blocked out her companion while she attempted to read the newcomer's mind.

Without a solid link, his thoughts were scattered and disorderly, but several impressions came to the forefront for Kira. The first was that he looked down on those around him—perceiving the other workers to be nothing more than menial cogs. Beneath that, he was working on something important. They were about to make history, and he'd get to be a part of it. The final impression was that whatever experiment was underway had a danger unlike anything else the man had previously encountered. Not only were the subjects dangerous, but he had to tread carefully with his own position.

'Subjects'? Are they doing experiments on people here, too? Kira was pulled back to the outside world by the sound of a plastic tray clanging to the ground.

"Sorry!" a woman said while bending down to pick up the

spilled contents.

Another woman chuckled and bent down to help her. "Collisions are bound to happen now and again, don't worry about it."

Kira had a moment of panic when she realized she'd lost sight of the man, but she quickly spotted him seated at the end of a table on the other side of the room.

Keeping one eye on him, she returned to her salad.

Leon gave her a questioning gaze from across the table. "What aren't you telling me?"

"Nothing I won't reveal in due time," she said around a mouthful of salad.

A slight shake of his head was Leon's only reaction. He resumed eating his sandwich in silence.

Kira finished her meal two minutes before the man across the room, but she remained seated until he rose to clear his tray.

She stood and grabbed her own tray. As she separated the waste into the appropriate bins, she timed her movements so she'd be able to leave right after the man.

"Go on ahead back to your office. I'm going to... stop by the restroom," Kira said to Leon.

He rolled his eyes. "You will do nothing of the sort."

"What did I say earlier about supportive statements?"

Leon threw up his hands. "Fine, but I warned you."

"I'll be careful." Kira jogged lightly across the cafeteria toward the hall where the man had gone.

She paused at the corner and peeked around nonchalantly. The tech was still going straight ahead.

Stepping as quietly as possible, she hurried down the hall to catch up with the man before he reached the next intersection. He took a right.

Kira crept forward and waited to see his next move. Her glance told her it would be obvious, since there was only one visible door down that segment of hallway. However, when she chanced a second look, she saw the back wall of the hallway pulling aside to allow the man through.

A placard on the hidden doorframe read: 'D Wing – Restricted Area. Authorized Access Only'.

Kira shook her head. *Those sneaky bastards.*

The door wouldn't stay open for long. She made a run for it.

After two steps, a firm hand caught her arm. Instinctively, Kira grabbed the wrist and twisted it to bring her would-be assailant to their knees.

"Ow, Kira!" Leon exclaimed.

"What are you doing here?" she hissed, releasing his arm.

The door was beginning to close. It was now or never. She took another step toward it, but Leon grabbed her again, looking into her eyes.

"Not now," he pleaded in her mind.

Fok, he's right. She couldn't go in without an exit plan. Kira groaned. *"Well, this confirms they're up to something."*

"And we shouldn't be here. Monica may decide she's had enough of your skulking around at any moment."

"Thanks for coming to find me! I got turned around," Kira said aloud, and Leon released her arm. She caught his gaze again. *"As soon as I figure out how to get in and out of there myself, you won't be able to stop me."*

CHAPTER 11

MONICA REVIEWED THE footage of Kira's near-infiltration of the D Wing. She scowled at the monitor.

"What do you want to do about her?" Jared asked.

"There's not much we *can* do," Monica replied. She rose from her seat with a huff and paced behind her chair in the observation room. Her plans for Kira had counted on having more time to prepare. Unfortunately, the Guard officer had proven more enterprising than Monica had anticipated.

Jared crossed his arms. "Detain her?"

"The Guard would come looking for her. We can't compete with the military resources of the extended Taran Empire."

He frowned. "So, our cover is blown. That's it?"

"No, of course I won't give up that easily. We need a subtler approach. I'm thinking." Monica continued her pacing.

With how easily people could be manipulated, there had to be an elegant solution. Kira herself was an important part of that equation. The strength of her natural abilities, coupled with her training, made her a prime specimen on which to test the penultimate stage of their experimentation. Unfortunately, that wasn't yet complete. They'd need one final push to bring their plan to fruition.

"I have an idea," Monica said to Jared as the plan formed. "It's not without its risks, but it's the best way to keep the operation on course. We've been on borrowed time since the Guard discovered our other lab."

Jared crossed his arms. "Forgive my bluntness, but why didn't you take additional precautions when you moved the subjects here?"

Her lips curled into a smug grin. "We have failsafes in place—no need to worry. And besides, the Empire's eyes were already on this system enough with the reunification agreement so close to being signed. We're trying to put on a friendly face, remember? Besides, Kira is exactly who we've been looking for."

"You intend to use her as the test subject for Stage Four?" Jared asked.

"She's perfect, don't you think?"

He nodded with consideration. "Already trained as a soldier… she'd probably put on a great show."

"It would be an excellent template to build upon. I believe our collaborators would be pleased." Monica placed her hands on the back of her chair, lost in thought.

"Have you ever met them—in person, I mean?" questioned Jared.

"No, but they pull some very powerful strings. If we deliver on our promises, we will be well compensated. They always take care of those who play their part."

"How will we get her out of here, though?"

Monica smiled. "Through the front door, of course."

"Assuming by that point we'll be surrounded by the Guard, how are we supposed to do that?"

"When I say our friends pull some powerful strings, you must trust that they are powerful strings indeed. I'll share my plan, and it will all be taken care of for us."

Her colleague let out a slow breath and nodded. "I trust our work and your word. Tell me what I need to do."

— — —

"So, what's the plan for today?" Leon asked as he turned off the car in the MTech parking lot.

"Probably not another trip to the gym after how I whooped your ass last night," Kira jested with a gloating grin.

Leon rolled his eyes. "It wasn't *that* bad."

Kira had to admit, he had kept up better than she would have anticipated. Leon had always been more of the intellectual type than a jock during their teenage years together—not that the two were mutually exclusive—but his recently acquired martial arts hobby had clearly done him good. She could tell he was raring for a rematch, and she had to admit she was looking forward to it herself.

For now, though, her attention returned to her mission. She stared at the lab's entrance, aglow in the morning light. "It's probably best you don't know my plans."

"That dangerous, huh?" Leon slumped back in his seat and unfastened the safety belt.

"I can't give you any specifics, knowing Monica is a telepath. Let's just say that I need concrete proof of wrongdoing in order to pull in the Guard without it turning into a political disaster."

"Have you been paying attention to the news reports?

There's already a major political upset underfoot with this system."

Kira had watched President Joris' address while she was getting ready in the morning. The call for peace and to recognize the authority of the Taran Empire aligned with her own political leanings, but she was saddened to see counterarguments pour in from commentators after the speech ended.

Her home system was fairly isolated compared to the core worlds in the Empire. While the three planets offered sufficient resources to maintain a good quality of life, their relatively low population would be an issue in the long-term. Exactly two college-level institutions existed in the Elvar Trinary, limiting career options, and the relative self-sufficiency required many people to take positions in manual labor or service. Given the level of technology available, everyone should have been able to pursue more advanced work, if they desired—but the imbalance in population relative to the necessary functions to keep their little civilization running meant many people were held back. Mysar had raised the issue on numerous occasions, but the gentle Elusian people were content to allow their future to unfold at a slower rate. They were very young worlds and still needed to find their own identity.

Rejoining the Taran Empire would supply some of that culture, and the resources necessary for balanced growth that would provide greater opportunities to all citizens. It was the greatest argument against the Mysaran's bid for independence and why they would unify in the end.

However, the path to get to that resolution was messy, as the birth of so many nations was. The Elusian president's words would not sway everyone. With any luck, those objections would subside once final agreements were signed.

"Those reports of Guard military action were proved to be false rumors," Kira replied after a moment of reflection on Leon's question. "The news outlets are making a big deal out of nothing."

"That's the news for you," he said.

"Just remember, I'm covert ops—whenever we can keep it that way, at least. Unless things go completely sideways, no one should ever know I was here."

"Monica already knows," Leon countered. "Every time you set foot in the facility, you put yourself at greater risk."

"I can handle myself."

"I don't doubt your ability to kick ass and take names. Stars, my shoulder is still sore from when you almost took me out yesterday."

She flashed a semi-apologetic smile.

He waved it off. "I'm fine."

But Monica is telekinetic, for foksake. She'd rip me apart with her mind, not dislocate a shoulder. Kira's doubts must have been written on her face, because Leon just raised an eyebrow and tilted his head in response.

"She might be dangerous," Kira continued. "But that doesn't change the fact that I need *proof* of what's going on in there. The Guard is counting on me to get the job done."

"Perhaps I can find someone on the inside who'll help you out…"

"Why didn't you mention that possibility before?"

"It didn't occur to me until last night. I got to thinking about what you said regarding the 'hidden' jobs—cleaning staff and the like."

"Right. What about them?"

"Well, I might know a guy. He has zero technical aptitude, and I was thinking any collaborators would need to have some grasp of the tech we were investigating, so he didn't come to mind. But this guy is all about keeping people fed and happy."

"Are you talking about a lunch server?"

"Indeed I am. Think about it—if there are people being held captive, they have to be getting some kind of nutrition. And that food needs to get routed through somewhere."

"You may be onto something."

Leon nodded. "We'll pay him a visit this morning." His face lit up. "Oh, and I got you a present."

A present? Please tell me this isn't for our three-day anniversary... "What for?"

"It's so terribly romantic—a privacy bubble."

"You mean a close-range cloaking module? That's military tech. Where did you—"

Leon shook his head and pulled out a palm-sized device from his jacket pocket. A seam ran around the perimeter of the metal rectangular object, adorned with a wheel and three buttons on one side. A tiny logo was on the underside.

"You forget that all military tech makes its way onto the civilian market in dumbed-down form," he said. "This one is used by ecotourists to get close to wildlife without scaring them off—it records a visual of the surroundings and plays that back along with noise-cancelling waves around a holographic static field bubble on a loop, so you can talk within it and from the outside it'll just look like you're sitting there. The loop won't hold up to close examination, but anyone glancing at a video feed shouldn't get immediately suspicious."

Some women might swoon for flowers, but Kira was a sucker for a good gadget. And pastries—Leon had nailed that one the previous morning.

She took it from him, noting that the operation looked identical to the Guard's devices she'd used throughout her career. "This is going to be so unbelievably handy. Thank you."

He tore his gaze away and stared out the windshield. "We should probably get inside."

"Right." Kira unbuckled her seatbelt and reached out to open the car door.

"Kira…" Leon grabbed her nearest hand, stopping her. "Be careful in there today."

She gave his hand a squeeze. "I will."

They climbed out of the car and entered the lobby.

With the cloaking module tucked into her pants pocket, Kira strode toward the security arch after Leon. He flashed his ID and passed through first.

When it was Kira's turn, the guard held up his hand. "The Director would like to see you."

Shite. Kira's stomach dropped, but she gave the guard a polite smile. "Really? She's already been so generous with her time."

Leon paused on the other side of the archway, looking uncertain about what to do.

"You go ahead," Kira told him, making eye contact. *"If you haven't heard from me by lunchtime, call the Guard,"* she added telepathically.

"I'll see you later," he acknowledged, trying to hide his worry but not quite succeeding.

"Where should I meet the Director?" Kira asked the guard.

"Head through the B Wing arch. Someone will meet you inside."

This is why I shouldn't bother making plans. Kira nodded her understanding and strolled across the lobby to the other arch positioned next to the reception desk.

"The Director asked for me?" she questioned the guard at the B Wing arch, and he gestured her through.

She held her breath while she passed underneath the scanner, but it didn't seem to flag her cloaking module. *Small blessings.*

Kira continued walking forward. A set of double doors automatically opened for her with a hiss, revealing an all-white hallway similar to the others she'd encountered in the rest of the facility.

A lone man with short, brown hair and gray eyes was walking toward her down the hall. "Kira?" he called out.

"Yes, hi." She recognized him as the scientist she'd seen in the cafeteria the previous day, whom she'd tried to follow into D Wing. *This can't be a coincidence.*

"I'm Jared," he greeted, extending his hand when he was close enough. "I work with Monica."

"Pleasure to meet you," she lied, and pumped his hand. "Monica wanted to see me?"

"Yes, she'd like to chat with you later about your test results. But first, I wanted to conduct a follow-up examination."

"What for?" Kira's tone had more bite in it than she intended, and she took a deep breath, putting on a smile that she hoped was friendly. "Sorry, didn't get sufficient caffeination this morning."

He chuckled. "We've all been there. I can get you a cup of coffee to sip on while we meet. This way."

Jared spun around and walked back in the direction he'd come from.

"Have you been with MTech long?" Kira asked while she fell into step beside him.

"Going on twelve years now," he replied. "This is my first opportunity to work with Doctor Waylon, though. She's something of a living legend in this industry."

I guess it makes sense when you have abilities few others possess and you aren't afraid to use them to your own advantage. Kira kept the thought to herself. "I take it you like working for her?"

Jared nodded. "I do. She has a commitment to fulfilling her vision unlike anyone else I've ever encountered. It's infectious."

This guy's all-in—no leaked information coming from him by choice. Fortunately, I don't need his consent. Kira nodded. "I appreciate someone committed enough to do whatever needs to be done."

They halted outside a door. Jared swung it open, revealing a windowless room with two chairs on either side of a table—similar to the first room where Monica had taken her the previous day.

"I'll grab you that coffee while you get settled," Jared offered.

"Nah, don't worry about it." Kira stepped inside. "I'm supposed to be on vacation, after all—I'll just take a nap."

Jared gave an abrupt nod. "Very well. Please, have a seat." He took the chair on the far side from the door for himself.

Kira eased into her chair. "So, what kind of testing is in order for today?"

"I'd like to run a detailed blood analysis. I believe that your telepathic abilities might be tied to a form of nanotech we've never been able to detect before."

That was new. "Nanotech, really? What makes you say that?"

"When I went over the results from your test involving the gerbil—"

"Yes, that…" Kira grunted.

"—I was surprised to see a… connection between you and

the rodent. While we knew such connections existed between life on Valta, the mode has been a mystery. This latest analysis used some new visualization technology. The differences are so minute that I'm not surprised they were missed in past research efforts. It revealed a sympathetic resonance between a unique structure in your and the rodent's brains, which I believe is responsible for telepathy."

That explains my hankering for carrots. Kira crossed her arms. "What does that have to do with nanotech?"

"I analyzed the gerbil, which was raised here, in comparison to those bred offworld. That structure is only present in life native to Valta—and upon further examination using the advanced imaging models, the structure did not have the same markers as the other organic material in the creature. This suggests that perhaps the structure is formed as a result of nanites existing throughout this ecosystem."

"Wait, you dissected him?" Horror spread across Kira's face. She'd done her fair share of killing in the Guard, but Mr. Fuzzers... Her hand clenched into a fist under the table.

Jared cocked his head. "Don't tell me you actually developed an affinity for the creature?"

No one talks about Mr. Fuzzers that way! Kira barely kept her fury in check. "I'm not big on killing creatures in the blind name of science. For food is one thing, but—"

"Oh, it was far from a meaningless death. The data we collected was very illuminating."

"I'm sure it was." Kira slipped the cloaking module from her pocket and set it in the center of the table so it could begin recording. "Now, what were you saying about this nanite structure?"

Jared ignored her question, staring at the device. "What's that?"

Just need to buy some time while it records enough to loop. Kira tried to sit as still as possible. "It's my optical stimulator for light therapy—space can get pretty depressing, you know. I need my treatment mid-morning and don't want to forget."

"A walk outside in the sun might do you well."

"Oh, I'm sure it would, but there's something I wanted to show you in here."

Jared's eyes flitted to the device. "Is it that?"

"What? Oh, no!" Kira forced a laugh. "That device has nothing to do with it—pretend it's not there. Actually, I thought it might be interesting for you to experience some of my abilities firsthand. That seems better handled in one of your labs, so I figured I wouldn't be outside at my normal treatment time."

"That actually does intrigue me." Jared leaned forward. "I'm curious about what you can do."

"What's easiest to demonstrate is a direct neural link."

He sat upright in his chair. "On second thought, this probably isn't the best time."

That's right, he should be worried. I can control him and he knows it. "Are you sure? I promise to be gentle."

His gaze drifted downward then back up to her face. "We should probably stick to my planned tests. Perhaps another time."

"That's a shame." Kira had been counting the seconds. It wasn't a ton of footage, but it'd have to be enough. "Well, I guess I can delay my treatment. I'll put this away so we can get started." She reached out for the device on the table and slowly drew it toward her, all the while covertly manipulating the dial on its side to trim the footage to the middle segment of the recording, from when they'd been sitting still. That way, the holographic projection wouldn't begin or end with her arm extending; hopefully no one was listening into the audio in the room. Once the trims were complete, she activated the cloak.

Her skin prickled as an electrostatic field radiated out from the device, followed by a second wave as the holographic outer layer and noise cancelling effect initiated.

"What the—" Jared was about to bolt from his chair, but Kira lunged across the table and looped her right forearm behind his neck, slamming his head down on the table. He grunted, dazed from the impact.

Kira took the opportunity to dive into his mind, locking him in a telepathic vise while she returned to her chair. She leaned forward with her palms flat on the tabletop. "What is in D Wing?" she asked both aloud and in his mind.

He resisted—more than most would be able to. Perspiration formed on his brow as he fought against the intrusion. "I won't tell you."

"I command you. What is in D Wing?"

His breath became ragged, gasping as Kira tightened her hold on him.

"Tell me," she ordered again.

"Research," he replied at last. "Genetics research."

"What have you done?"

"We created a new strain. The Robus."

The statement confirmed that the research was the same as that in the other MTech facility. Now all Kira needed was some tangible evidence so the Guard could move in. She may have been given authority to use any intelligence-gathering tactics necessary, but it'd be her word against that of a powerful organization.

"Where is the entrance?"

"There is one in each wing." A shudder ran through him as he fought to regain control, but he was powerless in her grasp.

"How do I get in?"

"A code and scanner."

"What is the code?"

He relayed a number string, then added, "But there is a biometric scanner. You'll never make it through."

Kira thought about her options. "Is there anyone watching us right now?"

He resisted answering, his eyes almost beginning to roll back in his head. "No, I was your designated monitor."

A smile crept across Kira's face. "Underestimated me again," she muttered. "All right, Jared, we're going on a little field trip."

CHAPTER 12

KIRA TIGHTENED HER telepathic hold on Jared as he struggled in the seat across the table from her.

"Wha…" Jared's words faded to a faint rasp. *"What are you doing to me?"* he questioned in his mind.

"Just controlling you the way I have no doubt you've been controlling your 'subjects' for stars know how long. And you're going to help me get everything I need to bring you down."

Hatred filled his eyes, accompanied by fear and worry. No, it was disappointment. This was a man who firmly believed in his work, however misguided it may have been. Kira could appreciate his dedication—she felt the same way about her own missions—but that didn't give him a pass. No one would get away with perverse experimentation on her watch.

"You're going to do everything I tell you," Kira told him. "If you try to tell someone anything is wrong, I'll compel you to gouge out your eyes and then slit your own throat."

He nodded. With her inside his mind, there was no doubt that he believed her.

"*Now stand,*" she ordered, switching over to telepathic commands since they'd be stepping outside. She was now firmly enough embedded in his mind that she didn't need to maintain constant eye contact.

Kira deactivated the cloaking field, an irrelevant cover after Jared had confirmed that no one was watching at the moment, and returned it to her pocket; it might come in handy wherever they were headed.

Jared unsteadily rose to his feet and stumbled toward the door.

"*Relax.*" She tried to send him soothing mental tones. "*No need to be concerned. I won't hurt you if you cooperate.*"

Kira checked over Jared's appearance. Fortunately, the whack on his head didn't seem to have left much of a mark, except for a little redness. It probably wasn't enough to draw attention.

"*Lead the way,*" she instructed.

Jared opened the door and stepped into the hall, his movements now appearing more fluid than they had initially. His innate twitchiness worked to her advantage, should any security guard happen across footage of them walking down the corridor.

The halls were empty. Kira walked just slightly behind Jared, as if he were leading her of his own free will.

He traced a path deeper into the facility, down two extended corridors.

Stars, how big is this place? The facility seemed entirely too large for the workforce she'd seen—or for the population of Tribeca, for that matter.

"*What are all these rooms?*" Kira asked telepathically when her curiosity could no longer be contained.

"*Storage,*" Jared stated.

At the risk of doing something out of character for someone on a tour, Kira tried one of the door handles, but it was locked. *"Open it."*

Jared complied using his keycard and handprint, his face twisted into a grimace of resistance.

Kira's chest constricted when she saw the contents of the room: racks of weapons. *What the fok?* She glared at her informant. *"What's going on here?"*

"Preparations."

"For what?"

"For war."

Well, yeah, that much was obvious. Kira bit her lip. *"Against whom and with what army?"*

"Anyone who resists," was all Jared told her in his mind. A spasm wracked his body. She couldn't push him further, lest she be unable to use him for the critical task ahead.

"What else do you have here?" she asked him, hoping for just a little more.

"Weapons, armor... soldiers."

Now, soldiers... that was what Kira was really after. *"Are those soldiers your test subjects?"*

Jared swallowed. *"Yes."*

"Where are they located?"

"In D Wing."

"Take me to them." Kira closed the door to the storage room, and it relocked automatically. *If this many rooms are filled with armaments, how many soldiers do they plan to have?* When she started doing the math, she didn't like the answer.

They continued down the hall. At a right turn, they reached a seemingly dead-end corridor similar to what Kira had encountered earlier in A Wing. *"Open it,"* she commanded.

Jared accessed a concealed control panel, placed his palm on it, then entered a code on the screen.

The back wall slid horizontally, revealing a corridor beyond.

"You won't get away with this," Jared managed to say in his mind.

"Spare me the cliché villain-speak. More leading, less hollow threats."

Beyond the false wall, the architectural aesthetic took on a decidedly different feel. Rather than shiny, white surfaces, the corridor was bare concrete. This was clearly an area that didn't need to keep up appearances about being a cutting-edge tech firm; it was strictly utilitarian.

Hesitantly, she followed Jared inside. The immediate interior was a four-way intersection, with sealed doors marked 'A Wing' and 'C Wing' to either side.

What concerned Kira about the bare-bones look of the place was that there were no signs of the supplemental amenities found in the rest of the facility, such as markings on doors to indicate maintenance crew storage rooms. It was entirely possible that the operations in this wing were wholly self-contained and she'd be on her own if she became trapped. While she was confident the Guard would come for her, she had no way to be sure they'd arrive before MTech did... whatever it was they did to people who didn't support their vision.

"Who has access to this wing?" Kira asked her informant, deciding that she'd rather know exactly how screwed she'd be if she was caught.

"Myself, Doctor Waylon, the Security Chief, and two caretakers," Jared replied inside his mind.

"Are we alone in here right now?"

"Yes."

"If yes, where are the others?" she asked.

"Doctor Waylon is in C Wing, the Security Chief only responds to emergencies, and the caretakers only come in early morning and night."

Kira relaxed her mental hold on him just the slightest measure, knowing no one was about to barge in on them. "And who or what do those caretakers look after?" she asked aloud.

"The subjects," he replied.

That's the ticket. "Take me to them," Kira instructed.

A grimace flitted across Jared's face, but he sped up his pace down the corridor.

The featureless outer corridor continued for one hundred meters before it took a bend. Ten meters beyond the turn, the hall opened into a square room that bore closer aesthetic resemblance to the outer areas. An island of computer stations was situated in the center of the room, and monitors lined the side walls. Doors were centered on the left and back walls.

Kira's heart dropped as her gaze passed over the monitors—those on the right wall provided a live feed of the activities in the outer facility, documenting all the places where Kira had spent time over the last day and a half. Whatever she had thought she'd gotten away with during her investigation, it was almost certain that they'd been watching and waiting to see exactly what she had been sent there to do.

She glared at Jared.

He nodded. "We know who you are and why you're here."

"Then why let me stay?"

"Because you're unique."

Before Kira could ask him to elaborate, she noticed the images on the monitors mounted along the left side of the room to either side of the door. "You fokers..."

The monitors displayed what must have been two hundred holding cells, half of which were occupied.

"How many people are here?" she demanded. *My team is going to lose their shite when they see this—probably Kaen, too.*

"We have one hundred subjects in this facility," Jared revealed, unable to answer her requests with anything but the truth.

"And what are you doing to them?"

"Making them more."

"Cut the mad scientist shite! What have you done to these people?!"

Jared took a step back. "We gave them a nanite treatment to enhance their innate abilities."

That was the previous stage of research Kaen indicated in the mission brief. So what are they really *up to now?* Kira glared at the scientist. "You're holding back, Jared. This will get very uncomfortable for you if you aren't honest with me." She tightened the vise on his mind.

He cried out in pain, gripping his head. His knees buckled, but he managed to remain standing.

Kira eased off. "What are you planning to do with them?"

"We began by administering a nanotech treatment that would express the desired traits, finding a way to merge the tech to allow expression of the alien physiology along with their telekinetic abilities. The intent, though, was to develop a new strain of nanites that will grant telekinetic skills to someone with no previous abilities."

Oh, fok... Kira's heart pounded in her ears. "They've been trying to solve the Generation Cycle on Tararia for years. You can't jumpstart the expression of telekinetic and telepathic abilities."

Jared smiled. "Maybe not with only the limited Taran

genetic stock. But those Taran scientists don't have the alien tech we do."

Kira swallowed. The MTech scientists had wanted her because she was 'unique'. She had no interest in sticking around long enough to find out how they wanted to exploit her. "Have you completed this new nanotech strain?"

Jared's face twisted while he tried to resist answering her question, but she stabbed a telepathic spear into his mind. "Over there!" he blurted out, pointing toward a door she hadn't noticed before.

"You first," she said, following him across the room.

The scientist grimaced when he reached the door and pulled it open.

A moment later, Kira understood why. Inside was a sophisticated laboratory like something out of a movie in the pre-Revolution records—test tubes, culture incubators, a laboratory glove box, and the obligatory array of microscopes and monitors displaying gibberish to Kira's untrained eye.

"This is where you keep all the secrets, eh?" she commented.

Jared grunted in response, wringing his hands.

"Where is the nanite strain?"

He shuffled across the room and grabbed a vial from a sealed case.

Kira snatched it from him. She held the vial up to the light. The contents were a slightly thicker consistency than water and had a metallic sheen, but it was otherwise unremarkable to the naked eye. "Will this work on anyone?"

"That's what the tests were to find out."

I can't let them use this. "Where's the rest of it?" Kira asked.

Jared was about to respond when a comm embedded in Jared's jacket chirped. "I'm coming back from C Wing. I'll see you in the lab."

Kira recognized it as Monica's voice. *Oh shite, I need to get out of here!* There was no time to do anything with any other nanite batches—frankly, she didn't even know how to destroy them. Getting the sample to the proper authorities had to be her priority.

There was just the problem of what to do with Jared.

"Out, now!" Kira directed him back out to the main room. She tucked the vial into her bra for safekeeping.

When Jared reached the island of computer stations, Kira nodded her head for him to sit.

"Now, Jared," she said, staring into his eyes, "I need you to forget everything we did here today." Even knowing that the man had done some horrific things, she still hated what she was about to do.

"I remember..." he murmured.

"Not for long." Kira dove into his mind, searching for his recent memories that had yet to be encoded into long-term storage. While it was possible to strip the deeper memories, as well, it was a much more time-consuming and delicate process. Since it had been less than an hour, taking care of his short-term recollections should be sufficient.

It took her a matter of seconds to find what she was looking for. She destroyed the memories related to entering D Wing and made selective edits to those related to their prior conversation, making it appear as though they'd chatted and he simply decided to leave.

Someone of Monica's skills would be able to identify the alterations, but, with any luck, it would take her some time to become suspicious. Kira just needed an hour or two.

To hedge her bets, Kira left a final instruction for Jared to begin an observation of one of his subjects. The task should delay him and stave off Monica's suspicion while Kira took care of her remaining business.

"Get to it," she told Jared, and then she took off at a jog toward the exit.

This better work, or I think I'll be the next one in a holding cell. Kira gulped.

She broke into a sprint down the straight corridor through which she'd entered, slowing only when she reached the security door. She briefly considered going straight to A Wing to meet up with Leon, but there'd be no log of her entering through the lobby arch, and it might flag her on the way back out. It was better to keep things looking as proper as possible.

Fortunately, no ID badge was required to exit, and the B Wing door began sliding open as soon as she tapped on an indicator mounted on the wall.

She peeked out into the hall. Clear—for now.

There was no knowing which hallways might be under surveillance by security personnel at any given moment, so she took a brisk but controlled pace toward the building lobby by following the exit signs. At last, she made it to the outer door.

Just as she had made it past the security arch, she saw Monica emerge from C Wing.

Kira quickly spun around to hide her face, but it was too late.

"Kira? Hello!" Monica called out.

Shite! Kira composed a pleasant smile and turned back to greet the director. "Oh, hi! I finished up with Jared and was just about to go see Leon."

"How did the test go?"

Oh, foknuggets. It's going to be pretty bomaxed obvious our conversation was cut short when there's no record of the test Jared was supposed to perform. Kira shook her head. "Please don't be disappointed, but I had a little too much to drink at dinner last night and I have a headache that just won't quit. I wasn't feeling up for telepathy. Tomorrow?"

Monica evaluated her. Kira could feel the other woman's prodding at the wall around her mind, but Kira held the shield firmly in place.

After several seconds, the director nodded. "Of course, I understand. Tomorrow will be fine."

"Thanks." Kira glanced toward A Wing. "Leon is waiting for me—there was some model he was excited to share with me."

"By all means. We'll talk later." Monica's eyes narrowed just the slightest measure as she inclined her head, then she walked toward the arch into B Wing.

Kira breathed a tentative sigh of relief and resumed her route to A Wing.

The security guard waved her forward but then frowned and held up his hand. "Ma'am, may I see that device in your right pants pocket?"

Why is the cloaking module a problem now *when I got through just fine this morning?* She slipped the metal rectangle from her pocket and handed it to him, making eye contact to persuade him with subtle trusting thoughts. "This? It's just for sightseeing—I'm heading straight out from here this evening on a tour."

The guard took the module, dropping his gaze to study the minute imprint of the manufacture's logo. "Ah, yeah. I did one of those when I transferred in. Have fun." He handed the device back to her.

"Thanks, I will."

He waved her through.

Letting out a long breath, Kira hurried down the main entrance corridor for the wing and followed the route to Leon's work area.

When she entered the open common space for the lab, three of the techs were working at the central computer stations and Leon was holed up in his office. She jogged to his office and tapped on the glass.

Leon looked up from his work and waved her in. "How'd it go?"

"Oh, it was lovely." Kira closed the door behind her and pulled out the cloaking module. She let it sit on his desk to record. "How's your morning been?"

"Great… you know, work-y," Leon replied. He looked into Kira's eyes. *"How long do you need for the loop?"*

"More time than we have right now." She activated the device. "We're in even deeper shite than I realized."

Leon sighed. "Why am I not surprised?"

"They're gearing up for a war," Kira said. "I don't know against whom, but they have all sorts of armaments, and I think the genetic engineering might be for some sort of super-soldier."

"Fok…" Leon breathed.

"What equipment do you need to analyze the programmed function of nanites?" she asked.

"Uh… That's not really my specialization," Leon replied.

"It gets to be now. Grab whatever you need. We're getting out of here."

Leon sighed. "Granted, I can figure out how to run an analysis, but that kind of analysis equipment isn't mobile, Kira. I'd need to use some of the stationary components in this lab."

"How long will it take?"

"I can probably complete a rudimentary assessment within half an hour."

That'll be cutting it close… With any luck, Jared wouldn't come to his senses before then. "Do it. Work as fast as you can—I need to know what abilities these soldiers may possess."

Kira pulled out the vial from her bra. "I got this."

"Fok, Kira! Where did you…?"

"I've been busy." She returned it to inside her shirt. "Get everything ready."

Kira deactivated the cloaking module while Leon grabbed the necessary equipment. When he returned, they refreshed the cloaking module to represent Leon's office with him working on the computer and Kira nowhere to be seen. In reality, she was camped out behind his desk out of sight from anyone passing by the outer glass wall exposed to the rest of the lab.

She knew she could have bolted, but the analysis was too important. The Guard needed proof to intervene as soon as possible—transporting a nanite sample for analysis, getting the results, and preparing for action would take two days or more. Those captives might not have that kind of time, if her hunches about Monica were correct.

"Analysis in progress," Leon told her in the safety of the cloaking module's field.

"I have a sneaking suspicion what it's going to say."

"We'll know soon enough."

Kira set her jaw. *No one messes with my home. If Monica thinks she can get away with this, she's in for a rude reality check.*

CHAPTER 13

ONLY ONE SUSPECT to go, and Kaen had more questions than answers.

In preparation for his final interview, Kaen had looked into the detailed personnel files for all three suspects. He hoped to corroborate their claims about when they were first approached by their mystery contacts, to see if there were any commonalities. Both the lieutenant and the captain had indeed been on leave three years prior, on the dates they claimed in their written statements. The lieutenant had passed through the station that supported Guard transit, when extra capacity was needed, and the captain had been passing through a station that handled tens of thousands of passengers.

The two incidents were within a day of each other. Kaen remembered that timeframe because the unit he was attached to had just completed a major op. They needed to route through the ancillary station while the nearby Guard base dealt with some repairs to the fleet. Never before had there been damage on a scale sufficient enough to mess up docking orders, but the Empire had been a mess during the governing Priesthood's fall.

But more than ships, they'd lost some good people on that op. It wasn't an occasion he'd soon forget. It was those events that ultimately precipitated his investigation into MTech and had set the tone for the last three years of his career. He now needed to see it through to the end.

Returning his thoughts to the review of personnel records, Kaen noticed that the third suspect—a comm tech named Reece Alan—hadn't left Guard headquarters during that same timeframe. That wasn't to say he hadn't been contacted at some other time, but it was a wrinkle in the near-pattern that had been forming.

Kaen sighed. *It's all still circumstantial. What is the thread that ties it all together?*

He didn't yet have an answer, but perhaps the final interview would reveal the clues he needed.

Olvera met Kaen outside the interrogation room, the same space they'd used for the previous two conversations. The other suspects were still being held in the brig until the investigation was complete.

So far, Kaen hadn't heard anything that would support leniency, should they be court martialed. They had been acting in accordance with a moral compass, but they'd still violated Guard procedure and were a security threat. Kaen wasn't happy that he would have to make the decisions that would dictate the fate of their lives when he was done with his investigation, unless he could determine for sure that their minds were under someone else's control. More importantly, he had to find out how to remove the foreign control.

"I hope this guy's got some better dirt," Olvera commented while she looked in the tiny viewing window into the holding room.

"Don't hold your breath."

Olvera flashed a smile. "You might be surprised what kind of crazy shite comm techs overhear."

He chuckled. "Want to take the lead on this one, Major?"

The security officer shrugged. "Yes, sir, I'll give it a go, if you don't mind."

"Be my guest." Kaen held out his hand for her to enter the room first.

The suspect, Alan, was seated at the table with his hands already cuffed to the securement bar. He watched Olvera and Kaen enter with wide-eyed distress. "Sir, ma'am, what's going on? They've been holding me for over a day, and no one will explain."

"I apologize for the delay in this conversation," Kaen began while gesturing for Olvera to take the sole chair across from Alan at the table. "We deferred this chat to see if any contrary evidence would surface, but I'm afraid the leak stopped as soon as you were in custody."

Alan swallowed. "I don't know what you think I've done, but I promise you I haven't done anything to hurt the Guard."

"Nothing is that isolated," Olvera said, taking over. "What may be innocuous to the Guard could have greater implications for the Taran Empire. That's why we have a chain of command. Break that chain, and there are problems."

"I've never broken chain of command, at least not knowingly," Alan insisted. "This must be some kind of misunderstanding. What do you think I've done?"

"No need to put on a show, Alan. We know what you did."

"I…" The helpless man looked to Kaen when he realized Olvera wasn't going to budge. "Sir, you have to believe me. I haven't done anything wrong."

Olvera folded her hands on the table. "Then how do you explain your user account being tied to secure Guard information being transmitted outside of our network?"

Alan's eyes widened further. "What? No! I'd never!"

"We have a record of the action, so that isn't up for debate. What we'd like to know is why you did it."

The comm tech shrank back in his chair. "I'd never betray the Guard like that. Either you were looking at the wrong thing or someone is trying to set me up."

"Can you think of anyone who'd want to frame you?" Kaen asked.

Alan shook his head. "Well, no... I mean, I've tried to be friendly, you know? We're family here. I try to get along with everyone."

A nice sentiment, but he's lying about something. He must be. Kaen crossed his arms and scowled at the captive.

The comm tech continued drawing into himself. "Who did the information go to? Maybe they could tell you more. They're the ones you should be going after!"

"It was routed to an MTech facility," Olvera revealed. "Do you have any ties to the organization?"

Alan thought for a moment, then shook his head slowly. "I've heard of them, of course, but I don't think I know anyone there. I'm not from that system."

"Have you ever visited there?" Kaen asked.

"No, never."

Olvera glanced back at Kaen then returned her attention to the suspect. "Do you have a history of memory loss?"

Alan paled. "Whoa, hold on! You're not suggesting that I did this and don't remember? That's crazy! I'm telling you, someone must have set me up."

"Answer my question, please."

"No, I don't have a history of memory loss. And you'll see I have a great service record and have always done my part for the Guard. I'm one of the last people you should be investigating."

Perhaps we do need to vet the evidence further. It is possible someone else was using his credentials. Kaen nodded. "We'll take your statement under advisement. Please understand that we'll have to hold you until this matter is resolved."

Alan worked his mouth but then bowed his head, shoulders rounded. "Do what you have to do, sir. But let me know when you find the real culprit, because I have a thing or two I want to say to them about messing with me like this."

Olvera stood. "We'll get to the bottom of this."

"Please hurry," Alan pleaded. "I'm going crazy cooped up in that cell."

"We're doing our best," she acknowledged, and then followed Kaen into the hall.

The two sentry guards entered to retrieve Alan while Kaen and Olvera stepped down the hall to debrief.

Olvera frowned. "You know, I think he honestly believes he's innocent."

"I didn't detect any deception, either. That doesn't change the fact that the data was transmitted using his credentials."

"Could someone have hacked his profile?"

"You know more about the security safeguards than me."

She nodded. "Well, it's unlikely, but certainly within the realm of possibility that someone used his account without his knowledge."

"Is there any way to confirm it was actually him?"

"There are internal cameras in all the communication rooms. We could pull up the feed covering his station and see if he was the one sitting there."

"Do it," Kaen ordered.

Olvera led him back to her office. She slid into her chair behind her desk to pull up the footage while Kaen remained standing.

After three minutes of navigating menus and searching through the security archive, Olvera located the right feed and displayed it on her main screen.

Kaen shook his head. There was no mistaking that the person working at the terminal was Alan. "It bothers me how easily he lied."

Olvera released a long breath and leaned back in her chair, steepling her fingers. "Like I said earlier, he does honestly seem to believe he didn't do anything. It doesn't come off like a lie if he thinks he's telling the truth."

"But he did it." Kaen pointed to the screen.

"What if he has no memory—or an altered memory?"

"That is the question, isn't it?"

"I didn't say there was a straightforward answer, Colonel. We have three events, each connected to politically charged situations that won't be easy to smooth over. Discovering these leaks was just the first step."

"The pattern, though…"

"Colonel, I'm no longer convinced there *is* a pattern. A few details line up in two of the cases, but that alone isn't enough to make a compelling argument."

"I'll give you that," Kaen agreed, "but those details also add up to more than I can ignore."

Olvera smoothed her hands over the pants of her uniform. "I want there to be a connection, too, because then it will all make sense. But sometimes, people just act for themselves. What I said when we started this investigation may be wrong—it really might just be coincidence. These could be three separate incidents that just happened to come to a head at the same time."

"Even if that's the case, how do you explain Alan's lack of recollection of his actions?"

"Maybe he was drunk-subterfuging?"

Kaen scowled at the security chief.

She laughed. "Sorry."

"I can think of half a dozen ways to explain memory issues, and none of them paint a very good picture. Someone wanted this covered up."

"It's like some evil alien overlord is messing with us tiny humans, just to see how long it takes us to go mad."

That's it! Kaen leaned against the cool, metal wall. He shook his head, letting out a weary breath.

"I'm joking." Olvera's brow knitted. "Wait, what is it?"

"These incidents all seem disconnected, but that was by design—you're right, we weren't thinking big enough. The commonality is that each deals with one facet of the system containing Mysar, Valta, and Elusia. Each incident addressed one of those planets."

"Okay, I agree that there are connections to the three planets within the same system, and that probably is a factor. But we still don't know what it's about."

"That system, of course."

Olvera sighed. "Well yes, but *what* about it?"

"If there are two opposing forces, then the target is most likely what's caught in between."

"Valta?"

"All the signs point back to that planet. We've known for years it's special."

"It is—no debate. How do the incidents connect? It might just be two sides playing political games against each other."

"No, after what I've seen, I think this is the work of a third party."

"Someone on Valta, perhaps?"

"No, more removed than that," Kaen said.

Olvera raised an eyebrow. "I really was joking about evil aliens."

"I won't rule out any possibility just yet. Somehow, that might be better than a rogue telepath mind-controlling Guard officers"

She nodded. "I don't get the motive. Why would these aliens, or whoever, be after Valta? Why fuel a civil dispute between Mysar and Elusia?"

"That is what remains to be seen," Kaen replied. "But Valta, for the time being, is the center of the action."

— — —

Monica strode into the observation room deep in the heart of D Wing. Looking around at the monitors, she noticed that Jared had gone to speak with one of the subjects in an interrogation room.

Just as well. I have an overdue chat of my own. She strolled into the corridor with the line of holding cells and stopped in front of her latest acquisition.

The man was in his thirties. With his thin build and prematurely aged skin from too much unprotected time in the sun, he hardly looked like someone with the fortitude to withstand the trials to come.

He inched back on his cot. "Why have you brought me here?"

"For some very important work," Monica replied, depressing the door control to slide it open. "Come with me." She telekinetically pinned the man's arms behind his back.

He gasped when he realized what she'd done, offering no resistance when she compelled him out of the room.

She directed him to an experimentation room with a clear outer wall and no furnishings. A thick, heavy body suit was laid out on the floor. Claw marks along the right wall gave clues to the room's previous occupants, and the man quaked on his feet, hugging himself. "What are you going to do to me?"

"Make you better." Monica extracted a syringe and the vial of nanites she'd been carrying in her lab coat pocket since morning. "Dress." She nodded to the suit.

"Why?"

"Do it," Monica commended, both aloud and in his mind. He complied.

While he was dressing, Monica drew the nanite solution from the vial into the syringe, what amounted to no more than four drops. As small a quantity as it appeared, when administered directly into his bloodstream, it contained enough nanites to permeate his body in half a day, so long as there was adequate fuel to aid in the replication. The specialized bodysuit would provide just that.

Gripping the clothed man in a telekinetic choke-hold, Monica inserted the needle into his jugular. She exited the room, releasing him from the telekinetic restraints when she pressed the door controls to seal him inside.

The man reached for his neck. "What was that?"

"Hopefully, the next phase of evolution." She smiled at him.

He held his hand over the puncture site and stumbled back toward the far wall. He collapsed against it then slid to the ground. Within seconds his hand had dropped from his neck, and he curled up on his side, falling fast asleep.

There were other ways to dose a recipient with the nanites, but the alternate methods took much longer to take effect. She didn't have any time to spare with this experiment. By morning, she'd know if the residents of Valta would be as useful as she hoped. While the nanites should be able to transform anyone, any opportunity to maximize those returns would be well worth taking.

There was nothing more to do with the man until then, so she headed back toward the observation room.

After five steps, her comm lit up with an automated security alert: someone had accessed restricted files. She had no doubt who it might be.

— — —

"Is it finished yet?"

"No, Kira. For the fourth time, the analysis is *not* complete. I'll let you know as soon as it is," Leon groaned.

Kira scooched back under Leon's desk with a huff. *How freakin' long does it take to analyze a bunch of nanoscopic technology that no one has ever encountered before?* She frowned. Even she knew she was being unreasonable.

"I'm sorry, Leon," she murmured. "I just want to get out of here. I keep expecting an army to walk in and grab me any second."

"Maybe you should go," he suggested. "I can finish up here and then meet you back at the cottage."

"No, absolutely not." She tried to give him a firm look of superior finality, but it was decidedly difficult from her hiding place on the floor.

Leon smiled down at her. "You're kinda cute when you're trying to be all tough."

"*Trying* to be? Let's not forget how I dropped you."

"I think you have some pent-up aggression you need to

release."

Kira thought about it. "You know, this *is* the longest I've gone in a very long time without sparring with one of the soldiers on my team. That makes for one exhausting workout."

Leon's smile faded. "That isn't some sort of euphemism, is it?"

"What? No! No, no, no. Those guys are like brothers to me." She tilted her head, eyes narrow. "Why?"

"Nothing."

A little jealous, eh? Kira concealed her smirk.

Leon came to attention. "Analysis is done!"

"About time!" Kira emerged from her hiding place just enough to view the computer screen.

"Oh… this isn't good." Leon paled.

Kira stared at the information on the screen, but it may as well have been alien code. "What? I have no idea what I'm looking at here."

Leon touched on some sequences in the analysis. "Okay, so I'm not a nanotech guy, right? I don't have a clue about how to break down the machines to their components and analyze what they're supposed to do. So what I did was something of a workaround. We have the different divisions of MTech, each with their own specialization. But we're an *integrated* company, so we need to know how those different components interact."

"Right, what about it?"

"I tricked the system. I told it I was working on a genetic model and needed to know how these nanites would impact my patient, since it would influence my genetic therapy treatment plan."

Kira sat back on her heels. "All right, that was creative."

"You can stroke my ego later. If this analysis is right, we

have a huge problem."

"Lemme guess… alien hybrids with telekinetic abilities."

Leon's jaw dropped. "How did you…?"

"There were suspicions based on some information we gathered at another MTech lab. And when I saw that they were holding telekinetically gifted people here, it was pretty much guaranteed that it was all connected. I also maybe sorta mind-read one of the secret researchers a little bit ago."

"Kira!"

"The details aren't relevant. This analysis is exactly what I need to get to the Guard so they can move in. Can you save it on an external drive?"

"They'll be looking for any drives leaving the facility. Those security arches work both ways."

"What about the hard drive on the cloaking module?"

"Yes, that could work." Leon reached for the device. "Stay hidden—and *quiet*."

Kira pinched her thumb and index finger and drew them across her lips while she tucked back under the desk.

Two agonizing minutes passed while Leon synced the module's hard drive and established a link to transfer the complex model. It was unlikely they'd be able to access the information on just any old computer, but Kira was confident the Guard would have the means to reassemble the data packet.

"Got it!" Leon whispered. "We can leave any— Oh, shite."

Kira frowned. "That sounded like an especially bad 'oh, shite'."

"The system just sent up a red flag. These sequences must have been marked to send a notice if they were accessed."

"What does that mean for us?"

"A bunch of really big, well-armed security guards are headed straight for us."

CHAPTER 14

"OH, FOK! FOK, fok, fok!" Kira scrambled to her feet.

"We can't be here, Kira," Leon said, his voice pitched with fear.

Kira pulled herself together. "Grab whatever you need. We need to get out of here!"

Leon shut down the equipment in his office and then they began marching as quickly as they dared toward the exit. No more than four meters outside Leon's office, they were stopped by one of the techs on Leon's team—Marty, based on his ID badge.

"Heading out early?" Marty asked.

Is he a stall tactic or just lonely? Kira didn't care to find out either way. "Sorry, I just came down with a major migraine and Leon is taking me home."

"Yeah, I'll drop her off then be right back," Leon said, playing along.

Marty frowned. "That's what's going on, huh? When I saw you crawl under Leon's desk, I thought something else was up."

Leon blushed. "Uh…"

"Maybe I worked myself into a headache." Kira wished she could have waited around to see Marty's reaction, but she took off at a brisk walk toward the exit.

Based on the redness of Leon's face, however, she guessed that Marty's jaw had hit the floor.

They broke into a jog as soon as they were out of the common area of the lab.

"Fok, Kira, that alert was tied to my work station. There's probably a hold on my badge."

She glanced over at him. "I'm not leaving you behind no matter what. You're a member of my team."

He nodded his understanding, but the worry remained on his face.

Footfalls from multiple pairs of heavy boots sounded from down the perpendicular hall between them and the exit.

Aaand there are the guards. Kira looked around for a potential hiding place and spotted a supply closet two meters ahead. She tapped on Leon's shoulder and pointed.

They bolted to it slipped inside, closing the door softly.

Just enough light leaked in from around the edges of the door for Kira to see Leon's rigid form. Standing a mere half-meter apart, she had the urge to hold him for comfort, but she didn't dare move a muscle.

She held her breath as the guards—she counted six—passed by, showing no break in their pace to indicate they'd spotted them in the closet.

After a count of thirty, Kira cracked the door open. The corridor was clear.

"Marty will point them back this way," she whispered. "It's now or never."

"What about my ID badge when we leave?"

"I'll take care of it."

Before he could question what she had planned, Kira made a flat-out run for the exit. Two strides short of the door, she dropped to a jog.

"Shite!" she shouted while she burst through the doors. "Why didn't you tell me what time it was?" She glared at Leon.

"Sorry?"

"Sorry won't cut it! I'm going to be late for my wildlife expedition. What kind of vacation is it if I don't get to go to the petting zoo?!" She stormed through the security archway. "Can you believe this shite?" Kira said to the security guard.

The guard looked at her, bewildered. "I wouldn't worry about it, ma'am."

"You too? All you men are the foking same!" she shouted.

To her relief, Leon took the chance to dart through the archway.

"I better make it by the check-in time, or you'll never hear the end of it." She gave one last glare at Leon for good measure and turned back to the guard to make sure he was still watching her and not his monitor. "And don't you *dare* pretend you don't want to snuggle with a baby cocobera!"

She spun back toward the door with a grand flourish and ran outside.

Leon ran after her, and they didn't slow until they reached his car. He used the remote unlock, and they piled inside.

"Wow!" he exclaimed while starting the engine. The car sprang to life, and he sped to the exit. "That was epic."

Kira wiped her hand down her face. "If Ari ever gets ahold of that footage…"

"Who's Ari?"

"One of the guys on my team. He's made it his personal mission to document my best moments and post them for all the universe to see."

Leon smirked despite the tension from the last half hour. "So I can find you online?"

Oh, fok. Now I've done it.

— — —

Monica scowled at the MTech Security Chief, Tucker. "What do you mean they walked out the front door? There was a flag on that account!"

"Yes, ma'am. There was apparently a… distraction," the chief replied with a quaver to his voice. He stood a full head taller than Monica, but he'd turned into a scared puppy the moment he saw her eyes flash behind her contacts.

"Then go find them." She emphasized each word, rising onto her toes.

Tucker took a step back. "I'm afraid our jurisdiction doesn't extend beyond the lab, ma'am."

Monica held in a curse. "Are you going to follow my orders, or do I need to go after them myself after I rip out your foking—"

"Doctor, what happened?" Jared wandered into the room, looking dazed.

She pivoted her rage to her assistant. "About time you showed up! What took you so long with that subject?"

"I'm… not sure." Jared swayed slightly on his feet and brought a hand to his temple.

Monica turned to face him. "What do you mean?"

"I…" He looked around, as though to get his bearings in a place that should have been familiar. "I went to see Kira, we talked, and then I went to interview the subject."

Monica frowned. His tone was too measured and

mechanical. "How did your talk with her go?"

"She… wasn't feeling up to the interview and left early."

That much matched up, but clearly that wasn't the whole story. "Jared, I need you to be honest with me." She looked into his eyes, using the pathway to bore into his mind.

The confusion Jared was expressing externally matched his inner thoughts. He was thinking about his most recent actions, and there was a clear memory of him outside one of the holding cells, but everything between their morning briefing and that most recent memory was… blurry.

Kira was good—very good—but this was a rush job. Frankly, Monica expected better.

"We've been compromised," Monica stated.

"What… how?" Jared asked.

"By you, obviously." She groaned. "Little Kira is bolder than I'd given her credit for. She must have taken control of you and implanted a memory in an attempt to cover her tracks."

"I wouldn't…"

"But you did, Jared. This is why we haven't tried to experiment on telepaths. They're too unpredictable. Fok!" Monica paced next to the computer console. This development was a wrinkle in their plans, but not a disaster.

Jared's face flushed with a combination of anger and embarrassment. "We'll find Kira."

"Tucker here was just saying how that's outside of our jurisdiction." Monica glared at the Security Chief.

"What did I do while I was under Kira's influence? We might have grounds for an emergency intervention," Jared said.

"I was just thinking the same thing." Monica accessed the nearest computer terminal and brought up footage from

Jared's meeting with Kira.

She watched as Kira placed a device on the table, and then the two occupants just appeared to sit there for two minutes.

"What were you doing?" she questioned Jared.

"I don't remember."

Then, Kira's arm suddenly withdrew from the center of the table—even though it had been at her side a moment earlier—and she and Jared rose from their seats and headed for the door.

"You weren't watching them?" she hissed at her security officer.

"I had one of my men watching, but it didn't seem out of the ordinary at the time," he replied. "There wasn't a physical altercation."

Monica swore under her breath. "And then where'd Kira go?" She searched through the other video feeds until she found the one for the hallway outside. "Well, that's foking great. You led her right here."

The footage ended when Kira and Jared entered the observation room—one of the few areas in the facility not under surveillance. Monica would have to extrapolate. "If it were me, I'd question you about what we were doing here, and then you'd point me to… the lab."

She glided across the room and opened up the secure room, going straight for the most prized item. Sure enough, a vial of the latest nanite strain was missing. "Fok!"

Had she any less control, she would have smashed everything in the room. Her hands balled into fists, nails digging into her palms. She took a deep breath in a vain attempt to calm herself.

"Bring her here!" she demanded as she stormed back into the observation room.

"But the authorization—" Tucker started to object.

"We have all the grounds we need for emergency action. Proprietary tech has been stolen from this facility, and we're within our rights to get it back." She stared down the two men. "But we're not stopping there. We have less than a day to complete this assignment, or all our years of research will have been for nothing. Round up everyone on the list you can find."

Tucker swallowed. "That—"

"We haven't received the results from the latest subject—" Jared objected.

"I don't want to hear another foking excuse! Submit the request to MTech HQ. We make a move tonight at 23:00. Get all the backup we can get."

"But—" both men began.

"Do it!" she screamed.

Tucker nodded his understanding and departed to issue the orders.

"This will paint an even bigger target on us," Jared said once they were alone. "The Guard will undoubtedly move in."

"Then let them."

"And if the nanites don't take?" Jared questioned.

"All we need is one viable subject to bring to our benefactors. One of them is sure to be what we need. It'll work. And if it doesn't, we'll still have the real prize."

"Kira?"

Monica's eyes narrowed. "Yes. She'll be sure to come, once she realizes we have her parents. We'll grab her then."

CHAPTER 15

KIRA'S HEART RATE had finally normalized by the time they parked outside her cottage. The peaceful little community had been a refuge from the danger she faced each day inside the MTech lab, but now she wasn't sure anywhere on Valta would be safe.

Leon seemed to be thinking the same thing. "They'll come for me, won't they?"

"MTech doesn't have jurisdiction outside of their premises."

"Like that'll stop them."

Kira couldn't bring herself to lie. "We stick together. I won't let anything happen to you."

"What can the two of us do against the entire MTech security force?"

"We're not alone." Kira climbed out of the car. "We'll call in the Guard and beat the shite out of anyone who tries to stand in the way of us rescuing those captives."

"And until they get here?"

"We watch each other's backs."

Kira opened the front door to her cottage and beckoned Leon to follow her. She jogged into the bedroom and grabbed her travel bag from where she'd stashed it in the closet. Tucked away in an inside pocket was an encrypted comm system.

She set it on her bed and sat down on the edge of the mattress while Leon looked on from the doorway. After activating the device, Kira waited for its signal to sync with the Guard's systems through the subspace connection.

"This is Guard Command," a woman answered. "Please confirm your field auth."

Kira stated her alphanumeric field identifier for the op.

"Greetings, Captain Elsar. What can we do for you?"

"I have the evidence in hand. Request immediate direct-action mission for hostage liberation and extraction."

The woman on the comm didn't reply for several seconds. "Transferring you to Colonel Kaen."

"Kira, what's your status?" Kaen asked after a ten second pause.

"Physically unharmed, Colonel, but my identity has been compromised and they're coming for me. MTech has definitely been up to no good. I have a sample of the nanites—about to send you an analysis." She pulled out the cloaking module from her pants pocket and connected it to the dataport on the comm system. Navigating to the appropriate subdirectory, she attached the files to an encrypted data packet and sent it on its way.

"What's the situation?" Kaen asked while he waited to receive the files.

"Their research is well into live trials. They have a number of people being held deep within the facility—around one hundred."

"And the facility defenses?"

"Light on personnel, but they've got enough small arms and ammo for an army stored in the facility. There's a choke point at the entrance, and artillery above the one and only door. Also, the facility director, Monica Waylon, appears to be a former TSS Agent trainee—though I haven't witnessed more than her telepathy for myself."

"Stars!" Kaen sucked in a breath. "I wouldn't have expected that."

"Me either, sir. That was no doubt a major factor in my cover being blown. I don't know how much time we have."

"We can have a team there by 05:00. Ah, receiving the data packet now," Kaen acknowledged

He was silent for a minute while he reviewed the analysis. Then, he let out a long breath. "I'm no geneticist, but even I know to be scared by this shite."

"Yes, sir. It's terrifying to think about what soldiers like that could do."

"If the hostages have indeed been 'turned' into one of these Robus, they may not be entirely themselves. This might not be a situation where the hostages greet us with open arms."

"We're Guard, sir. We can handle anything," Kira replied. "But you'd better send the powered armor."

"You'll get all the soldiers we can muster and the best tech we have to get those people out unharmed. I'm coming there myself to oversee the extraction."

Kira glanced over at Leon with surprise. "Sir, you're coming here?" She hadn't known him to go into the field for years.

"After what I've been dealing with here, this one needs a personal touch," Kaen replied. "See you at 05:00. Check in at 23:00 to confirm our landing coordinates."

"Acknowledged."

"Guard Command out."

The connection terminated.

Kira rose from the bed and took a deep breath. "I hate that we have to wait until morning."

"What more can we do?" Leon said. "We're two people. You've seen what they have in there. I'd be next to useless, aside from maybe hitting someone over the head with a chair, and we'd be going against a group of possibly unstable alien hybrids that may or may not have an insatiable lust to tear our faces off."

"That's a little melodramatic, isn't it?"

He sighed. "You know what I mean."

She gave him a reassuring smile. "We need to make ourselves scarce until tonight, in case they come looking for us."

"You did say something about the petting zoo," Leon replied. "Though, I guess we should avoid the place you said we were going."

"Like Monica would believe that for one second. That actually sounds like the perfect cover. We'll pay with physical currency and keep our heads down."

He brightened. "All right. Let's get you some quality time with a baby cocobera."

Kira grabbed her travel bag. "Let's go."

They made the drive into the countryside outside of Tribeca to the nature preserve with the most tourist activity. Staying in a crowd was likely the best way to stay safe for the time being, so Kira had no qualms about losing herself in play with the fuzzy baby animals of her native world. The animals of Valta had always had a natural affinity to her, being a telepath, and Kira soon found herself the envy of the tourist children when she got the most attention.

The park closed to visitors at 17:00, so they were forced to head back to civilization. In the interest of staying in a well-traveled place, they went to the town center and did some window shopping before getting dinner at one of Kira's favorite restaurants from her youth. By 22:30, they were one of only two couples left in the restaurant. They needed to move on.

Kira considered finding a hotel or some other place to wait out the night, but everywhere she could think of was too inhabited; if MTech came for her, she didn't want to worry about civilians getting caught in the crossfire. Her own cabin was fairly isolated, and she already knew the lay of the land. All in all, it wasn't a bad place to hunker down for a few hours of rest. With the scheduled check-in time approaching, they headed back.

When they arrived in the residential neighborhood, Kira instructed Leon to stay by the car while she checked out her cottage to make sure there were no unwelcome visitors. She scouted the perimeter and saw no sign of forced entry, then did a sweep inside. For good measure, she also examined Leon's place. Both checked out.

"I can't wait until this is over," she groaned after meeting up with Leon and retrieving her travel bag from the trunk. "If there's anything I hate, it's not feeling secure in the place that's supposed to be my home base."

"I don't know how you deal with this on a regular basis. Two days, and I already feel like I've had enough," Leon admitted.

"You've been handling the situation really well."

"I buckle down when I have to."

"You do. I've always appreciated that about you." Their

eyes met for a moment, but she tore her gaze away. "Well, those cocobera are adorable, but that musk really lingers. I'm going to clean up and change."

Leon looked down at a paw print on his pants. "Yeah, I should do the same. I'll meet you back here in fifteen for the call."

"I don't think we should split up," Kira said. "Safety in numbers and all that. I'll go with you to get your stuff. We'll get cleaned up at my place where there's less clutter that might hide surveillance tech."

After Leon gathered some items, they returned through the darkness to her cottage. Though there were no signs of anyone lurking nearby, she couldn't shake the feeling that they were being watched. They both searched for intrusive monitoring equipment inside Kira's residence, but turned up nothing. As far as Kira could tell, the place was untouched.

Feeling more secure about their location, Kira quickly showered then dressed in casual pants and a fitted long-sleeve shirt. She waited by the comm system while Leon got cleaned up.

"Nothing yet," she reported when Leon returned to the bedroom, looking refreshed. "Should come through any minute."

Sure enough, forty seconds later, the comm lit up with an incoming communication. "This is Guard Command. Please confirm your field ID." It was Kaen's voice.

Kira stated her identifier again.

"All right, Kira, we're in transit. I have confirmation from local authorities for a landing site between Tribeca and the MTech lab. It should give us a good position to get into all the places we'll need to be as quickly as possible. Sending the exact map now. Is there anything else you need?"

"Just my team and my suit," she confirmed.

"You've got it. See you at the landing site at 05:00. Guard Command out."

Kira opened the map and showed it to Leon.

"I know the place," he said. "I guess now we wait."

She nodded and tucked the comm equipment away.

They went out into the living room.

Thinking about the op, Kira found her anger from earlier returning. "It sickens me to see people taken advantage of like this."

"I feel that way, too. But the best thing we can do for them right now is wait for your friends at the Guard to arrive so we can take care of this properly."

I hate being helpless! These telepathic abilities don't count for shite when it comes to a fight. Her heart pounded in her ears. "Those captives might not have all night. Monica could—"

"Yes, they're in danger, but we can't single-handedly do anything to save them. We'll hunker down here for the night, just like you said. Stay together. I can't in good conscience let you do anything else so reckless that *you* might get hurt," Leon said. He placed his hands on her shoulders.

She tried to look away, but he bent his head to catch her gaze. "I've already spent too long with regrets about what I should and shouldn't have done with you. I won't add another."

"Leon, this isn't the time."

"This is exactly the time. I don't want to lose you again."

Her throat constricted. "You deserve so much better than what I gave you."

"There are a lot of things I could have done differently, too."

"No, you were perfect. You gave me space when I asked for

it, but I stupidly shut you out. I should have included you in the conversation. To join the Guard and only give you a day's notice..."

He cupped the side of her face. "I'm sure you did what you felt you needed to do at the time."

"It was unfair."

"It was. But it didn't change how I felt about you. Stars know I tried."

Kira was at a loss for words as Leon gently brushed his hand across her cheek. She still remembered that touch—had been craving it ever since she left home so long ago.

His violet eyes conveyed all his fear and worry for the danger they faced. And, deeper, the love he still felt for her, even after all this time.

Searching within herself, she realized she still felt it, too. It was why she'd never moved on—not truly—with anyone else, and why she'd always been afraid to come back home to this place.

"The Guard..." she managed at last.

"Is there some regulation against you having a relationship?"

"No."

He searched her face, leaning closer. "Then why fight this?"

She didn't want to, not anymore. "Leon, I—"

Shouts of fear sounded in the distance.

Kira snapped to attention, pulling back from him. "Did you hear...?" She ran to the window.

"Yeah. What—" Leon followed her.

More shouts sounded, followed by a loud bang of metal on metal.

"Shite, what's going on?" She peered into the darkness, searching for the disturbance.

"There, those lights." Leon pointed through the gap between two houses to the left.

Sure enough, lights were bobbing between the houses one street over. Based on the height from the ground and the speed, Kira could hazard a guess for what they were up against. "I think that's an assault mech!"

Leon's face drained. "As in armor and guns and—"

"Stop gawking. We need to run!" Kira grabbed her bag containing the comm and dashed to the door.

"I'll get the car," Leon called to her.

"No, it's too conspicuous. We go on foot." They bolted through the door and took off at full speed away from the cottage.

Behind them, sounds of the mech's rhythmic steps were accompanied by shouts from people, some barking orders and others crying with fear.

Kira wove between the cottages in the opposite direction from the commotion, trying to stay in the shadows. Leon stayed close while they ran, only slowing occasionally to check over his shoulder for any sign of pursuit.

When they reached the edge of the residential neighborhood, Kira deviated from the main road, into the brush. She had a vague recollection of the area from when they'd driven by in the car, and if she remembered correctly, the brush gave way to thick forest sixty meters from the road.

Her eyes began to adjust to the dim moonlight now that they were away from the inhabited area, and she could see the edge of the forest ahead. *Just need to get to somewhere we can regroup. We'll figure it out,* she assured herself.

The brush transitioned into ferns once inside the forest, and vines hung in their path. The thick tree canopy blocked most of the moonlight, so Kira had to rely on feel to move forward. *What I wouldn't give to have night-vision goggles right now...*

She slowed, picking her footing carefully. After five minutes of gingerly moving deeper into the forest, she saw the faint silhouette of a felled tree that had all the makings of a good camp bench.

"This should be hidden enough," she said to Leon, keeping her voice to a whisper.

"What's your plan?" he whispered back.

"I... don't have one yet. I figured they'd send their security people—total asshats, by the way—after me, or us. But a midnight mech visit wasn't something I'd anticipated."

Leon's frown was just barely visible in the dappled moonlight. "So why were they going after other residents?"

Kira ran her hand along the log to make sure there wasn't anything squishy, and then crouched down behind it, using it for cover as she rested her arms on top of it. "That depends on who the 'they' are. I'd normally say that it would have to be military to have a mech like that, but I saw one at another MTech facility."

"You think MTech might be going after civilians?" Leon's voice was laced with fear and worry. "Our families..."

"They may have just been conducting a search, since there'd been a security breach. Why we weren't the first stop, I don't know."

"Or they're taking people."

Kira hadn't wanted to admit that possibility to herself, but deep down she knew it was the most likely. "As much as I want to go back and see what's going on, getting ourselves caught won't help."

Leon crouched down next to her. "That's a reversal."

"Well, you were right earlier. And that's the one time you're going to hear those words uttered in that order, so savor it."

He chuckled and extended one arm around her.

She leaned her head on his shoulder. "We have a little over five hours to make it to the rendezvous point. It'll be a significant hike on foot, especially since we'll need to move slowly in the dark."

"I know some back roads with good brush cover that'll get us there."

"Having a local contact does come in handy."

"I wish we were going to head away from the danger, rather than toward it."

Kira patted his knee. "A Guard soldier is almost always running toward the conflict."

"I'm sure I'll get used to it."

Kira looked up at him. "We should probably finish that conversation we started, once we're not in immediate fear for our lives."

He dropped his arm from around her. "Yeah, of course. I didn't mean—"

She found his hand and entwined her fingers in his. "Just because I can't think about it right this second doesn't mean I don't want to."

Leon relaxed. "Good."

"I know it will take time to regain your trust."

He squeezed her hand. "I can be patient."

"All right, to be continued." She savored the contact for a moment longer before returning her attention to the present. "For now, our priority is to stay out of MTech's sight and get to that rendezvous."

"Running from MTech..." He shook his head. "I can't believe I ever trusted them."

"I would have, too, in your position. We grew up with their

innovations keeping us safe from the time we were kids. And I doubt the *entire* organization is corrupt—most of the people working at the local lab here are probably doing good work that will help people across the galaxy."

"While a handful are hurting hundreds instead. And now they may have gone after our friends and family…"

Kira placed her hand on the side of his face and gazed into his eyes. "We'll get them back. Don't worry."

He nodded and took a steadying breath.

She stood. "We should get closer to the Guard's landing site. We can find another place to hide once we arrive."

"Right." Leon rose to his feet and brushed off some moss from his pants. "We should be able to make it in two or three hours. The path I have in mind is the long way around, but I'd rather not come face-to-face with one of those mechs."

"I fully endorse this plan. I've already been shot at once this week, so my quota is filled."

Leon sighed and set out into the dark.

CHAPTER 16

ELLEN REVIEWED THE latest coded message that had arrived while she slept: >>*It is almost time. Soon the Guard will move against Mysar, and you will have your opportunity to take action against the Elusian president. Be ready.*<<

She cleared the sleep from her eyes and sat up in bed. The years of preparation had all come down to the coming moments.

Her stomach lurched with the thought she'd soon kill a man who'd been a leader and mentor to her, but she knew it was for the greater good. She needed to protect her home at any cost.

— — —

Leon's route on the back roads proved to be a more strenuous slog than Kira had anticipated. Three hours passed under the moonlight while they hiked along the side of the road, ready to dive into the bushes and tall grass a pace away if they spotted anyone approaching from across the valley's flat terrain.

"Are you sure you know where you're going?" Kira grumbled, swatting at insects that had been circling her for the past kilometer.

"Yes, we're almost there," he insisted.

"That's what you said an hour ago."

"This time I mean it and I'm not just saying it to placate you."

Touché. Kira shut her mouth—more to keep bugs from flying in than because she was done grousing.

They tramped along in silence for another half hour before Leon finally halted. "That clearing over there," he pointed toward a field on a low hill half a kilometer to their right, "is the location indicated on your map."

"Finally!" Kira checked the time on the comm; it was coming up on 03:30. "And with more than an hour to spare."

"You should never doubt my punctuality." Leon smiled, but it was clear he was tired.

"Let's find a little hollow where we can rest," Kira suggested. She wasn't thrilled about the idea of going into a combat scenario on no sleep, but that's what stims were for. Even a short nap was better than nothing, though.

"That should be a good spot ahead." Leon indicated a grove of trees one hundred fifty meters from the landing area.

"Perfect."

They left the side of the road and slipped into the trees. A small interior clearing offered just enough room for them to lie down on the ground.

"You rest, I'll keep watch," Leon told her.

"You really don't have to—"

"I'll get to kick back and watch everyone else do all the work once the Guard arrives. Rest." He sat down cross-legged.

Kira dropped her bag next to him, and she reclined with her head propped on top of it. Leon stroked the top of her head while she got settled on the uneven ground, then allowed her to nap undisturbed.

She drifted in and out of consciousness while she struggled to filter out the sounds of nighttime Valtan wildlife, but she bolted awake the moment she heard the rumble of approaching engines.

"That sounds like a Guard landing craft," Kira said, shaking off her grogginess.

Leon was on his feet, gazing up at the sky. "It's big."

She rose and stood next to him, following his sightline to the craft descending through the wispy cloud cover. "A big craft to hold the big guns."

After checking to make sure no items had dropped out of their pockets while they had been seated on the ground, they left the grove and headed for the vessel coming in for a landing. Output from the ship's thrusters flattened the surrounding grass, and Kira held Leon back until the engines wound down.

Within a minute, a broad door in the side of the craft dropped open. The first people to emerge—already adorned in powered armor—were Kira's team.

She beamed at them. "About time you showed up! I've had an insufficient dose of minion-bossing in my diet."

Seeing that the surroundings were safe, Nia removed her helmet. "That would explain why I've been feeling so empowered…"

Ari and Kyle slipped off their helmets.

"Sounds like you got yourself in the middle of a right proper mess," Ari commented, eyeing Kira.

"Yeah, well, things were going too well. Had to ensure our job security." She grinned at him.

"Who's your friend?" Nia asked while looking past Kira.

"Right." Kira waved Leon forward. "This is Leon Calleti, my local contact for the op. We go back a long way."

"Uh huh…" Nia cast her a knowing look, a smirk playing on her lips. "Well, nice to meet you, Leon. Nia."

Ari and Kyle introduced themselves in turn.

"Fair warning," Kira said, "the three of them don't mess around, so if one of them calls dibs on the last piece of cake, let them have it."

Leon swallowed. "I'll keep that in mind."

Nia smiled sweetly. "And it goes without saying that we look after each other. If you mess with Kira, we'll take it personally."

"Yay, everyone's met and we're all best friends!" Kira held up her hands in a mock cheer before turning serious. "I need to talk with the colonel." She headed for the landing craft's door.

Leon cautiously passed between the soldiers as he followed Kira. "Are they always that intense?" he whispered to Kira while they walked up the ramp.

"What, that? That was nothing. They must get a good feeling from you—the last guy they thought was trying to get into my pants ended up cowering in a corner within thirty seconds."

"Holy shite…" Leon breathed.

Kira shrugged. "Yeah, relationship didn't work out."

At the top of the ramp, she spotted Colonel Kaen and Major Sandren going over orders for a group of forty soldiers in powered armor.

"…and remember, there are civilians in there, so be selective with your fire," Kaen was instructing. "We risk our lives so others may live in peace. Let's get Valta back into the rightful hands of its people."

"Sir," Kira greeted.

"Captain, I'm glad you made it," Kaen replied with a nod, turning toward her.

"It's been a crazy night." Kira sighed. "There was some sort of raid on the town. Not sure if it was MTech or Mysaran military, but we think they took additional civilians—either as hostages because they knew you were coming, or as test subjects."

Sandren scowled. "They must be desperate, to make that kind of public move."

Kira nodded. "The captives they have in there—we can't assume they'll all be friendlies."

"Understood," Kaen said. "The order is non-lethal force wherever possible."

"Yes, sir. I'll get my gear on." Kira awkwardly reached into her bra. "Oh, and this is the sample of the nanites I collected from the lab." She handed it to Kaen.

"Thank you," Kaen acknowledged, tucking it into a compartment on his armor.

"What about him?" Sandren asked while examining Leon. "We could use his insights into the facility layout."

"Oh, I really don't—" Leon began.

"The facility is very segmented," Kira cut in. "I've probably been to more areas than Leon at this point. I suggest he waits back here, and let the soldiers handle it."

"Very well, but gear up," Sandren instructed. "I won't have a stray blast take anyone out if one of the teams brings any action back this way."

Leon took an unsteady breath. "Right, of course."

"Everything's in here." Kira passed by the rows of armed soldiers toward the craft's prep area, and Leon followed her.

Passing by a supply cabinet, Kira grabbed a couple of protein bars, knowing she'd need fuel for the fight ahead. She handed one to Leon.

"I didn't think I'd be anywhere near the fighting," Leon said, ripping the package open.

"If we do our job well, you won't be. Armor is just a precaution." Kira checked that no one was nearby, then whispered, "I would like to keep you in one piece." She bit into the bar.

"I'll do anything that helps me stay that way." He smiled back.

Kira found her newest set of powered armor propped in a nearly empty rack inside the prep area. There were six other backup suits, and she located one that would be the best fit for Leon. After finishing their snacks, she detached the weapons, since Leon wasn't rated to fire them, just leaving the armored body shell and helmet.

"You ever been in something like this before?" she asked him.

"No, never."

"Well, it's straightforward. It'll augment anything you do. The pressure sensors for grip are pretty smart, so you don't have to worry about accidently crushing bones if you go to shake someone's hand—unless you push it. When you make a movement, if the sensors detect excessive force, they'll automatically stop. You can override them by continuing the action, but it will stop at each step."

"Got it," Leon acknowledged.

"Walking is easy—just take a natural stride and the gyros will balance the suit. If you break into a flat-out sprint, a spring system will kick in to boost your speed—your legs won't actually move any faster, but each stride will cover *a lot* of distance. I wouldn't recommend trying that on your first go around."

"Considering my plan was to sit quietly in the corner, I don't think that will be a problem."

"Sounds good to me." Kira popped off the helmet and pressed the load button on the armor's chest plate. The torso, arms, and legs split open to receive an occupant. "Come on, step in."

Leon slowly backed into the armor, positioning his arms and legs to match the angle of the suit's limbs. When he made contact with the back interior, the armored plates folded around him. "Whoa!"

"Oh, yeah. Should have warned you that it pressurizes. These work as EVA suits in a pinch, but they're not rated for long-term vacuum exposure."

"It… tingles." Leon stood still with his arms out at an awkward angle from his sides.

She mounted the helmet to its holding clip on his left shoulder. "Move around. The pressure will adjust."

He circled his arms and took a cautious step. Then another. "Okay, this really isn't that bad."

Kira smiled. "That's the spirit."

She hurriedly donned her own armor, which had been custom-fitted for her. The suit included some stealth tech that wasn't standard on all combat armor, though it was looking like she wouldn't get to put that to use until the next op. This one was going to be a firefight, despite their best intentions. She checked the charge on her plasma rifle and stowed it in the designated slot on her back, and she then grabbed a multi-handgun for the holster on her thigh—one of her favorite weapons, capable of firing kinetic rounds and sonic blasts to daze enemies. Two concussion grenades in her belt and some extra kinetic rounds completed her loadout.

"Ready?" Kira asked Leon. She mounted her helmet to her shoulder until she got the comm frequency for the op from her team.

"Good to go."

They exited the prep area. Upon returning to the open space at the top of the ramp, they found it empty. Kaen's voice carried from outside, so they descended the ramp.

"Ready for duty," Kira said to Kaen and Sandren when she spotted them on the grass several meters from the landing craft.

"Good, almost ready to make our move," Major Sandren replied.

"What do we know about the situation, sir?" Kira asked.

"It looks like this might be related to a larger political move. Someone seems to want a conflict to escalate between Mysar and Elusia," Kaen explained. "The Mysaran government is taking the Guard's presence here as a sign that the Elusians are only signing the reunification agreement with the Taran Empire so that we'll take out Mysar and claim this whole system for ourselves." He paused, a grimace flitting across his face. "While we were landing, I received a confidential tip that Mysar has launched a battleship toward Elusia."

Sandren looked at the colonel, eyes wide. "I'm shocked they'd do that."

"How long before it arrives?" Kira asked.

"At its current speed, seven hours. But that trip can be made in far less time if they boost hard," Kaen said.

"Oh, shite, I have to warn Ellen!" Leon exclaimed. "Have you told Elusia about the ship?"

"Until the unification agreement is signed, we can take no official military action. We're skirting the rules enough by being here on Valta." Kaen shook his head.

"What about an *unofficial* notice?" Leon pressed. "My sister works in the president's office."

"Their people deserve time to prepare for an attack, if there is going to be one," Sandren chimed in. "I think a tip like that is just what's in order."

Kaen deliberated for longer than Kira would have expected, but he eventually nodded. "Do it. You may use the comm room on the landing vessel, but be sure to tie the message to a local civilian code."

"Yes, sir!" Kira raced with Leon back up the ramp.

"I never wanted her to take that job," Leon muttered. "Politics in this system are such a mess."

"That's probably why she took it, you know. She wants to make a difference."

"I guess you two always did have that in common."

When they reached the communications room, Kira dismissed the comm tech and created a civilian-coded feed, like Kaen had instructed. "Do you know your sister's direct contact?"

"Yeah." Leon entered the necessary information on the screen.

"Okay, this should just take a minute to connect." Kira initiated a vidcall. She checked the local time in the Elusian capital; it was 10:15 local time, so she should be available.

After thirty seconds the call connected, and a woman in her early thirties matching Leon's hair and eye coloration answered. "Hello, this is— Wait, Leon? Is that you?"

"Hey, Sis," he greeted with a smile. "Remember Kira?"

"Wow, yeah... What are you doing back on Valta?" Ellen asked.

"Long story," Kira replied. "We're calling to pass on some

information that you need to get to the president. It didn't officially come from us."

Leon's tone turned solemn. "The Mysaran Coalition launched a battleship that's headed for Elusia. It will likely show up on your scan soon, but we wanted to give you as much advance warning as possible."

Ellen's face drained. "No, that's not possible. This isn't how it was supposed to go…"

"I know it's difficult to believe that it's come to this after years of trying to find peace, but you need to have the people of Elusia prepare for a potential attack," Kira urged.

"No, you don't understand." Ellen shook her head.

"Ellen, the media has it wrong," Leon told her. "Whatever you think you know about what's been going on the past few days, it's not the whole story."

Her brow knitted. "What do you mean?"

"The specifics are classified, but let's just say that the Guard *definitely* isn't making a military move against Mysar," Kira replied.

"Stars…" Tears filled Ellen's violet eyes.

"Sis, are you okay?" Leon asked.

"I think I've been played," she murmured.

Kira examined the other woman on the screen. "What are you talking about?"

"I was sent to Elusia to get close to the government." Ellen wiped a tear from her cheek. "My… my role was to take out the Elusian president."

"What?!" Kira and Leon shouted simultaneously.

"I'm not going to go through with it now, obviously. But the plan was to assassinate him and blame it on the Guard, undermining the reunification agreement to keep the entire Elvar Trinary out of the Empire."

Kira's stomach turned over. "That's a pretty foked up plan."

Ellen ignored the comment. "I'll talk with the president and see if we can stave off an attack and keep things from spiraling into a worse political nightmare."

"Good luck. Talk to you on the other side," Leon said and ended the call.

"Assassinate the president? Is she out of her mind?!" Kira exclaimed.

Leon scoffed. "That is not the woman I grew up with."

"Shite, me either." Kira took an unsteady breath. "I can't wait to get the fokers who've orchestrated this madness."

"That makes two of us."

Kira stepped toward the door. "All right, let me give Kaen and Sandren the update. We need to shut down that lab."

CHAPTER 17

ELLEN STARED AT her desktop in silence. *I just admitted I was about to murder a head of state.* Hearing the words out loud had made her realize just how misguided she'd been. Assassination wasn't the way to bring about a better future.

She reached for her desk drawer, realizing that her hands were shaking. Inside was the syringe she'd been given by her secret contact for the purposes of the impending deed. She'd hidden it under a stack of hardcopy reports no one was likely to go looking for. The slim, metal case looked like something an old-fashioned fountain pen might be presented in as a gift. Ellen pulled the box from its hiding place and examined the contents. It was just like she'd left it.

No, someone has been playing me. I can't trust one side over the other. Everyone has their own agenda. I'm not helping my world if I'm just a tool in some sick master plan. She rose from her desk and dropped the case and syringe into a hatch set on the back wall, which led to an incinerator—one perk of being in a government office dealing in sensitive information. *I won't use this. Not now or ever.*

Ellen took several calming breaths. It was time to really make an impact.

She left her office with nothing in hand and took the elevator to the level housing the president's administrative suite.

Nico was in his customary position behind the reception desk. "Hi, Ellen. I don't have you on the president's calendar for today."

"It's an urgent matter—can't wait," she said, not breaking stride.

The two guards outside his office tensed as she approached.

Ellen spread her arms. "I have critical information regarding Elusia's safety. Please let me pass."

The left guard held up his finger and then knocked on the door. He stuck his head inside and said something. After five seconds, he swung the door open and gestured Ellen through.

"Thank you." She nodded to him.

Inside, the president was seated at his desk. "Ellen, what information do you have?"

She closed the door behind herself. "Sir, I'm sorry to interrupt."

Joris frowned. "We're in the middle of a crisis here. If this is a new issue, I'd rather not know yet."

"It's connected—regarding the Coalition. They've sent a battleship toward Elusia."

"No! They wouldn't…"

Ellen swallowed. "This isn't an official tip, but it's coming from a source I trust. They wanted to give us time to prepare."

"Whoever your friends are, we're indebted. I'll reach out to the chancellor right away and see if I can get to the bottom of this." He activated his desk.

"That's not all, sir." Her stomach turned over.

"I'm listening."

"Sir…" Ellen searched for the words. There was no right way to put it—may as well go all-in. "Sir, I originally was sent here to kill you."

The president's face drained. "What?"

Ellen held up her hands to show she was unarmed. "But I'm not going to do that. I realize now that I was manipulated into thinking about my world as an individual entity and that remaining isolated was the best way forward. I believed that with all my heart, and much of me still does. But I've come to believe that there are powerful forces working behind the scenes to pit Mysar and Elusia against each other. For what end, I have no idea. But I do know that the only way we can stand up to an opponent like that is by unifying, not separating."

Joris' hand hovered over his desktop. "I should call security on you."

"I'll understand if you do. But I beg you to trust in my conviction to save my world."

He studied her. "We both share the Elusian ideals of peace and goodwill—and forgiveness. But this…"

Ellen lowered her hands. "I didn't have to say anything about my original mission, but I couldn't move forward with that weighing on my mind. If we're to work together going forward, I want it to be based on a relationship founded in trust."

"You never gave me a reason to doubt you. You played your role well."

She shook her head. "You made it easy to follow you, sir. Elusia is lucky to have a leader like you, and they need you more than ever right now."

The president took a slow breath. "Against any advice I'd receive, I'll give you the chance to regain my trust. It took courage to come clean."

"Thank you, sir." Few would have such forgiveness in their heart. If anyone was worthy of her enduring loyalty, it was him.

Joris motioned to the chair across from him. "Sit in on this call with the chancellor. I could use another set of ears."

— — —

Allowing his would-be killer to remain in his presence had put President Joris in an odd mood. On the one hand, it saddened and terrified him to think that this woman he'd trusted for two years had only worked her way into his employ so that she could end his life. On the other hand, he was humbled that she'd alter long-held convictions because she believed him to be a worthy leader. He'd need time to process the development, but right now he had to focus on finding out why the Mysaran Chancellor had authorized a battleship to advance on Elusia.

"Pay attention to her wording," Joris instructed Ellen while he prepared the video call. "We need to determine if she's lying, subverted, or just really does hate us that much for whatever reason."

"I'm ready," Ellen confirmed.

Joris activated the connection. *Let's hope she even picks up.*

He watched the call status on the desktop readout. It had been acknowledged by the chancellor's administrative assistant and appeared to be on hold. *Come on...*

Fifteen seconds later, the call was accepted in the chancellor's private office.

Chancellor Cynthia Hale's dark brown hair and pale green eyes were almost as opposite to Joris' as their personalities. "President Joris, I'm surprised to hear from you."

"Really? I thought one of your battleships heading for my planet was a worthwhile reason for us to have a chat."

"What?" She shook her head and cracked a smile. "You must be joking."

"According to my scan data, it's no joke at all." *Stars, I hope Ellen's contacts had this right—we have no scan data or physical proof.*

The chancellor leaned forward, her hands folded on the table. "Joris, I can account for all of my ships. Can you?"

He faltered. "You know Elusia's space military barely has a ship between them."

"And Mysar's is not so large that one battleship could go rogue without me knowing." She looked down, then back up at him. "I have confirmed—as I already knew—that they are all in their respective berths at the stardock or on patrol. If there's a ship heading toward you, it's not one of ours."

"Chancellor, please forgive the accusation. My information—"

"You have always distrusted us." Hale's eyes narrowed. "I wonder if perhaps we shouldn't claim your planet and be done with this."

"Cynthia, we both know—"

"Oh, so first name familiarity, eh? Not this time, President Joris. I know the Guard is staging at Valta. This was all a distraction so you can make a play for Mysar. Well, we're not going down without a fight, that's for sure." She ended the call.

Joris slumped back in his chair. He glanced at Ellen. "No, I don't think I need a second opinion on that."

Ellen looked ill. "Sir, I would trust those who told me that information with my life."

I'm not sure how much value she puts on a life, given what she was going to do to me. But he didn't see deceit in her eyes.

"Your contacts may have been misled themselves. Maybe this was the real plan all along."

"Stars…" Ellen hugged herself.

"We only have one option." Joris took a deep breath. "I need to sign the reunification agreement with the Taran Empire."

"Right now?" Ellen paled further.

"We need immediate military support. If Mysar wants war, I want the biggest military we can get."

— — —

All told, sixty new subjects had been added to Monica's collection. Unfortunately, not a single one of them had responded to the first treatment in the way she'd hoped, nor had the man she'd tested earlier that day.

"Worthless! Every one of them. They have all the same markers. Why isn't it taking?" she mused aloud, not expecting a response.

"I think I've identified the problem," Jared replied from the adjacent workstation. He had dark circles under his eyes from working through the night, but his passion was stronger than ever. Probably trying to make up for giving away all their secrets, if Monica had to guess.

"What is it?"

"We missed one sequence in our splicing. The nanites are still looking for one telekinetic marker in order to activate. We need to strip out that remaining reference, and then it should work."

There were thousands of lines of genetic code programming within the nanotech. It wasn't surprising they'd overlooked one tiny segment. "Except it's worthless to us without a subject. It'll take two weeks for the existing batch to clear from the subjects' blood. I was so certain it would work…"

"I was, too. I'm sorry I let you down again."

"Oh, Jared, a pity party will win you no favor. Redeem yourself through the work."

"Yes, ma'am." He turned back to his station. "I'm completing the corrections now. We should have a new batch of nanites ready within half an hour."

"Finally, some good news."

The question remained, however, for who to test it on. Subjects were all disposable, but she was running out of time and needed to maximize her investments.

While Monica could use just about anyone—perhaps even Jared, himself, if she got desperate—she'd much rather find a native Valtan. If her estimations were correct, such a person would possess far stronger abilities than someone with no innate extrasensory abilities. A Reader, in particular, would make a most excellent prototype to bring to her benefactors, even if that would be over-selling the product a bit. After all, that was the nature of sales.

Monica still had her eye on one Reader who she'd be all too eager to turn into her pet. And if the Guard landing vessel parked a kilometer away was any indication, Kira would be walking right through the front door and into her hands any minute.

CHAPTER 18

"BEAST MODE ACTIVATED," Kira said with a grin to her team, detaching her plasma rifle from her back.

"Be careful in there." Concern filled Leon's face, but his tone was confident, making Kira feel even more energized.

Nia cast another appraising look between Kira and Leon. "It's the enemy that should be worried."

"They've messed with the home of someone on the best tac team in the whole foking Tararian Guard." Ari's eyes shined. "And we won't stand for injustice."

Kyle laughed. "You sound like a recruitment ad."

"I would make a *great* spokesperson, and you know it," Ari replied with a grin.

"Or there's Kira's latest video entry," Nia offered.

Kira rolled her eyes while she grabbed her helmet from the mount on her shoulder. "I have a very long memory, my friends. Payback is cumulative."

"It's all empty threats. Secretly she likes it," Kyle said.

"I guess you'll just have to wait to find out." Kira slipped on the helmet, and her vision was replaced by the view on her HUD. "Comm test?"

Her team slipped on their own helmets and sounded off.

"Check clear," Kira acknowledged. She turned back to Leon and activated the external speaker on her armor. "See you soon."

He nodded. "I'll be here."

Kira returned the suit settings to internal comms and then loped down the hill in the direction of the MTech lab. Her unit and three other teams of four fanned out in formation.

Another two dozen Guard soldiers had gone ahead to scope out the opposition from inside a tree grove that stretched between the landing area and MTech. Her team slowed as they entered the trees, eventually arriving at the other side of the grove near the MTech entrance. The advance teams had taken up positions along the tree line.

Kira pressed her back against a tree with sightlines to the entry door and peered around the trunk. The lab's parking area nearby was now occupied by a matte gray transport ship. Two military assault mechs were patrolling the entrance, accompanied by eighty visible soldiers, plus the automated assault gun on the roof.

"Well, those weren't there before," Kira said on the private channel to her team.

"Yeah, figured you probably would have mentioned that," Kyle replied.

"What do you think—MTech private security or Mysaran military?" she asked.

Nia peeked around her own tree. "Tough call. I don't see any distinguishing marks on the ship or mechs."

"My guess is mercs," Kyle chimed in.

"I'm inclined to agree," Kira replied. She switched over to

the common band for all teams present. "Looks like the welcoming committee sent us our favorite kind of gift basket. Let's go for a meet and greet, but try not to damage the goods."

Acknowledgements lit up on the periphery of her HUD. She took a deep breath and centered her mind. "Go!"

As one wave, the forty Guard soldiers dashed across the darkened plain toward their target.

The mechs' thermal sensors picked them up first, and they pivoted their mechanized firing heads toward the group. Each fired an RPG, but the team's distributed formation made the mechs' aim ineffective, and the grenades detonated on open ground between two soldiers.

The Guard soldiers shook off the blast and continued their charge.

Enemy mercs opened fire with a mix of kinetic rounds and plasma blasts, illuminating the battlefield in a purple electrical glow. With the strobing weapons fire, the action unfolded in freeze-frame motion before Kira's eyes, and her HUD adjusted to minimize the fluctuation in light level.

She spotted a clear path to the right that would take her near some rock formations, and she sprinted down the hillside, firing at the ground near the enemy mercs in the front line to drive them into a tighter clump.

Sensing that the grenades hadn't hit their marks, the mechs switched to plasma beams. Two beams shot out from each mech, slicing scorched trenches through the ground.

Foking beam weapons! Kira dove and rolled to the side to barely avoid one of the glowing beams as it crisscrossed in a random pattern across the field.

Her powered armor's integrated electromagnetic field could deflect plasma fire for short durations, but more than one full second of exposure and the nanocarbon would turn to useless goo.

Kira leaped to avoid another beam arc and took cover behind a boulder protruding from the ground five meters away.

She took aim with her plasma rifle around the edge of the boulder, firing a shot into the rotator plate between the first mech's upper weapons array and main body. The mech lurched backwards as a shower of sparks and smoke erupted.

The second mech pivoted its beams toward Kira's position. *That wasn't part of the plan!* She ducked behind the boulder just in time to avoid a clean plasma sweep through the air where her head had been moments earlier. The rock wouldn't last another three seconds.

"I need some cover!" she shouted into her comm, then dashed out from behind the boulder to the left.

Her team responded in force, laying waste to the second mech and then finishing off the first.

The next critical target was the gun on the roof—no armor-melting plasma rounds, but a couple high-powered ballistic rounds could be even more dangerous when their aim was true.

Kira strafed diagonally toward the entrance door. Her fire combined with the team's quickly tore the gun to shreds.

Seeing their main line of defense deteriorating, most of the armored mercs pulled back to the main entrance door, but others held their ground; some brave souls even began advancing toward the approaching soldiers.

"Non-lethal shots," Kira reminded her people over the common channel. They switched over to handguns.

The soldiers took aim with sonic blasts, but the mercs appeared to have in-ear comms, and the weapons had no effect.

Just had to make things difficult! Kira switched her

handgun to kinetic rounds and ran to a rock twenty meters from a group of five mercs who'd opted to seek cover in some shrubs. *Bad move, fellas.*

Kira lined up a shot using the aim assist on her HUD and fired a kinetic round, catching one merc in his right thigh.

He dropped to the ground with a yelp, scrambling to get his rifle back in firing position. His comrades looked around wildly for the source of the shots while she let loose four more shots. If these guys were military, then the Mysarans' armor had nothing on the Guard's. Unfortunately, shooting the mercs in their legs only served to immobilize them. She ultimately needed them unconscious, but so long as their comms remained in, the sonic stun mode on her weapon was useless.

Two of the mercs squeezed off poorly aimed shots in her direction, having finally located her, and she shot both of them in their dominant arm.

Kira cycled through the comm frequencies until she spotted an active channel not controlled by the Guard. *This must be them.* She opened a link. "So, I really don't want to hurt you because I know you're just the hired help, and probably underpaid, at that. If you want to take out your comms, I'll just knock you out and we'll call it good. Otherwise, I'll put a bullet in each of your arms. Up to you."

One merc laughed. "Is this a foking jo—"

Kira shot him in his right arm. "No joke."

He let out a cry of agony and ripped out the comm earbuds with his good arm. His companions followed suit.

"There! Now that wasn't so hard, was it?" Kira shouted at them using her external comm. She switched her handgun to the sonic pulse mode and fired.

They dropped to the ground.

The rest of the Guard soldiers had already dealt with the remaining mercs around the door. Kira ran toward one of the mercs who was still conscious, having been at the periphery of the sonic blasts' cone. She kicked his rifle away from where it had fallen next to him.

"Who do you work for?" Kira asked, pointing her handgun in his face for good measure.

"MTech hired us!" The man cowered with one hand in the air while the other gripped his bleeding knee.

"Yeah, no shite. But who are *you*?"

"My name is Anders," he replied.

Kira groaned. "No, who do you work for? Mysaran military, merc…" She couldn't form a direct link in his mind due to the full helmet on her armor, but she sent out a subtle telepathic prompt to facilitate his response.

Anders swallowed. "We're mercs, but my unit is Mysaran ex-military. We've been stationed in a moon base for three years—get a call out on ops now and then, like today."

"Always for MTech?"

"Recently, yes, but there have been others. I don't remember the names."

His tone indicated he was speaking the truth, so Kira released her hold on him and removed the pistol from his face.

"Time for a new career," Kira told him.

Twelve Guard soldiers were working their way through the mercs, applying stasis cuffs that would anchor them to the ground, with their hands and feet tethered behind their backs. It would be uncomfortable with bullet wounds, but that's what they got for resisting.

Kira handed over the merc she'd questioned to her comrade and met up with the rest of her team at the entry door. Well, what was left of the entry door. The previous engagement had shattered even the ballistic glass and left scorch marks and holes along the once-pristine back wall.

"That's convenient." Kira walked right in.

— — —

"Shite! What are we going to do?" Jared paced across the observation room, distracting Monica from her work.

"Let them come. This is a necessary phase of our plan," she soothed.

The newest test subjects were locked in their holding cells, useless to her after the mistake with the latest nanite strain. Monica needed her new subject to come looking for her.

But first she had to lull the Guard into a false sense of security. They'd need a challenge to overcome—a distraction to make them feel victorious so that the next phase could unfold just like she and her collaborators had planned.

"Release the Stage Two subjects," Monica instructed her companion.

"But they... We'll be ripped to shreds! And then they'll be on the loose!"

"We'll barricade ourselves in the back lab and then wait for the heroes to arrive. They'll take care of the rest." She calmly rose from her seat and strolled toward the sealed room.

Jared sat in stunned silence.

"Or stay here. I don't really care," Monica added.

He hurried after her.

All they needed was one viable sample; that was the deal with the collaborators. Once Kira was transformed and had a grasp of her abilities, she could be presented as the deliverable that would ensure Monica's bright future. All of the pieces were almost in place.

— — —

Colonel Kaen didn't like the way things had gone so far. It was one of those hunches he just couldn't shake—the kind he'd gotten on critical ops his entire career. But this... this was even more intense. He was certain this was one mission for which he shouldn't be on the sidelines.

Needing to clear his head, Kaen excused himself from the communications hub set up outside the landing craft.

He released a long breath and began pacing toward the far side of the ramp. As he came around the slope, Kaen spotted Leon Calleti staring into the dark in the direction of the MTech lab.

"Can't see much from here," Kaen said by way of greeting.

"Yeah, I know." Leon sighed. "I don't want to be in there, but I also don't like being left out here."

"You care about her, don't you? Kira."

Leon swallowed. "I'd given up on ever having anything with her a long time ago, but now I'm not sure what the future holds."

"Didn't quite expect that turn when I set her up with you as the local contact for this op," Kaen said with a chuckle.

"Maybe it was inevitable."

"Well, if you go down that route, you'll need to get used to her being in situations like this."

"I know. That prospect doesn't thrill me, but we can't have career decisions control all aspects of our lives."

"Guard *is* life, for many."

"And for Kira?"

Kaen shook his head. "Kira will always find a way to have what she wants. If that's you, you're a lucky man. And if she decides that you're dirt under her fingernails…" The colonel chuckled softly. "In that case, I wouldn't want to be you."

"We'll see what happens after this is over."

"Indeed."

They stood in silence for a minute, staring into the dark.

"We could use you in there," Kaen said. "Once we have the access codes from the director, you'd be an asset to help navigate the computer network and retrieve the relevant information. No one on my team is particularly versed in genetics or nanotech, so it'd be difficult to know what's important."

Leon hesitated. "Kira told me to stay here."

"Once the all-clear is given, it'll be perfectly safe."

"All right," Leon agreed after a short pause.

Kaen nodded. "I'll tell you when. Standby."

CHAPTER 19

THE MTECH LOBBY was clear, but Kira knew that Monica wouldn't have only one line of defense. "There have to be other mercs," Kira said over the internal comm system to the soldiers inside. "Not that it was an insignificant force out there, but that transport ship can hold way more."

"The facility is set up in wings, correct?" Kyle asked.

"Yeah, behind those three doors there," Kira pointed to the access points around the lobby, "and the hidden D Wing. My guess is the additional mercs are camped out in each of those corridors."

"Waiting for us to go in?" Nia speculated.

"If they're smart—" Kira cut off when she heard the telltale clink of a concussion grenade hitting the tile floor.

She dove to the ground, facing toward the exit. A blast rippled through the air, rattling what remained of the windows. The pressure wave caused the inner padded layer of her armor to cinch protectively around her.

Kira landed hard and skidded across the floor. Her armor

filtered out the worst of the grenade's punch, but her ears were ringing slightly. She looked behind her to see where the weapon had come from and saw that the door to C Wing was ajar.

"C Wing!" she shouted over the comm. "Anyone hurt?"

Acknowledgements lit up on her HUD that there were no injuries, and the soldiers dispersed around the lobby to find the best line of sight to the enemy.

Kira pressed her back against a concrete support column and took a quick look at the enemy's position. She moved her head back behind her cover and then brought up the still image on her HUD. The door to C Wing was now half open, indicating that mercs were likely behind the two partially open doors to either side of the passageway. Given the fortress-like construction, the doors were likely rated to withstand the kinetic weapons she had on hand; however, concentrated plasma fire was sure to do the trick.

While the intent was to limit casualties, force needed to be met with force.

"Let's drive them to the back of the hall. It ends in an elevator, so they won't have far to go," she told her team.

She grabbed both concussion grenades from her belt clip and lobbed them through the opening. *That ought to send them running.*

A second later, Kira heard a stampede of footsteps as the mercs retreated further into the corridor. The grenades exploded just inside the opening.

"There's no exit! May as well come out now with your hands up," she called to the mercs while the debris settled. No response. "Well, I offered."

With a signal over the comm, the Guard soldiers released a barrage of sonic blasts, advancing toward the open corridor.

To Kira's consternation, she didn't hear any mercs drop to the floor. "They might have sound-cancelling comms in," she told her team, switching her gun to kinetic rounds.

She was about to reposition to get a better look down the corridor when a miniature armored assault mech sped into view from down C Wing. *You have got to be kidding me!* Without hesitation, Kira whipped her plasma rifle from her back and fired at the mech.

Her team had done the same, and the gun mounted to the top of the mech became a glowing molten mass. Disarmed, the mech reversed its treads and zoomed back into the corridor at full speed.

Shouts rang out from the corridor, followed by a crash, an explosion, and the screech of rending metal.

What the...? Kira peeked from behind the support column. No mercs were visible, so she switched her handgun back to the sonic setting and advanced.

The C Wing entrance was in ruins, with a black scorch mark running its entire length where the molten mech must have rubbed against the surface as it sped past. Two mercs writhed on the ground with burns, and moans from others indicated that there were more injured further along in the corridor. Kira removed the comms from the two barely conscious mercs near her and knocked them out with a blast from her gun.

Ari and Nia passed her by to scout the hall.

"Oh, shite!" Ari exclaimed from ahead.

With the two mercs disabled, Kira ran to meet him.

Her eyes widened when she saw a pile of mercs to either side of the hall, seemingly torn apart by a frag grenade—and a mech-shaped hole in the elevator doors.

"Shite..." Kira breathed. "Did they try to blow the thing

up?"

Nia shook her head. "Looks like it. Got themselves instead."

Kira inspected the two piles of mercs but didn't see any life signs. "Tough break. Should have come out when I offered."

"I'm not sure that could have gone worse for them." Ari let out a long breath then nodded toward the elevator. "Think it's still operational?"

"Might be. We should disable it," Kira suggested.

With Ari's help, she pried open the doors and found that the elevator car wasn't on their level. She shined a light from her armor downward to find the mech crumpled four stories down. "That's not going anywhere."

For good measure, Kira blasted the guidance track in the wall of the elevator shaft with her rifle.

The plasma blast instantly melted the metal at the back of the shaft, making it impossible for the car to rise if there was anyone still down there. Presumably, there was access to the area through D Wing; they could go searching for survivors that way.

"Nothing left to worry about here," Kira announced. "Let's go for the rest."

Upon re-entering the lobby, she skirted the front reception desk for cover. She gestured for one of the Guard soldiers behind a support column near the front door to blast the doors with a specialized breaching gun he had custom-fitted in his armor.

A projectile flew from his armor. White goo radiated from the impact site, rapidly coating the door. When the surface was covered, the substance solidified in an instant, shattering the metal.

Cries of surprise sounded from the corridor within as

MTech's mercs backed away from the opening.

Kira sent out three rapid sonic pulses from her handgun, stunning the mercs—who apparently only had in one earpiece for their comms, presumably so they could better listen for the inevitable attackers. The mercs dropped to the ground.

Guard soldiers ran in to clear the fallen enemies from the corridor and secure them.

While they worked, Kira scanned the corridor for any signs of additional mercs, but she saw no heat signatures or electrical signals beyond the environmental norm. "Looks like this one is clear."

"We have movement in A Wing," Ari announced.

The doors parted with a hiss, and then a man shouted, "Don't shoot! We're coming out."

"Surrendering?" Kira asked over her suit's external comm.

"Yes!" the merc said, coming into view. "We heard what was going on out here... and we'd rather not get shot in the arms."

Kira lowered her weapon slightly while still keeping it trained on them. "Seriously, guys? Where's your professional integrity?"

He shrugged. "We're not getting paid enough for this shite."

"I respect your honesty." Kira waved him forward with her off hand, and he was followed by another six men and five women.

"What are you going to do with us?" one of the women asked.

"Lock you up out front until we're finished here, and then there's a major and a colonel outside who probably want to talk with you," Nia replied. She waved the mercs toward the exit with her gun.

They were received by a team who applied the securements around their hands and ankles.

"Yeah, this is way better without a bullet wound," the first male merc commented.

"Smart thinking." Kira gave him a thumbs-up. She switched back to internal comms. "All right, time to move in. We'll lead the charge into D Wing," Kira instructed her team assembled in the lobby. "We'll go through B Wing, since I know that route best. I'm passing the map now." She transferred the instructions over the secure connection.

"Hopefully there aren't any more of those bomaxed mechs lurking inside," Nia mumbled.

Kyle chuckled. "But they make for such good target practice!"

Kira stowed her rifle and readied her multi-handgun on the sonic blast setting. "Focus, team." She led the way toward B Wing's arch.

Like the rest of the lobby, the arch had sustained damage during the shootout. Sparks flickered as Kira passed through, but it still let out an angry beep accompanied by a red light.

She smirked behind her helmet's faceplate. "I think they already knew we were here, armed and dangerous."

"Effective system," Ari jested.

Kira swung what remained of the doors wide and propped them open with the nearby debris to facilitate a swift exit, should they need it—or for their backup to run in.

The white halls were silent and empty. The soldiers used the external comms on their suits to call out every dozen meters, in the event a captive was being held somewhere. There were no replies.

Kira peeked inside several of the supply rooms to check the weapons caches she'd observed on her previous investigation, but nothing seemed to be out of place. However, with so many storage rooms throughout the facility, it was impossible to know if other places had been used to arm the mercs.

After four minutes, Kira's team reached the seemingly dead-end corridor that led to the secret D Wing. Opening that door would be slightly more involved than anything around the lobby.

Nia evaluated the wall. "I say we just blow it."

"I guess we're already in pretty deep with the property damage. One more hole won't hurt." Kira backed her team up.

She and Ari fired their plasma rifles, cutting a crude archway clear through the wall. The reinforced material was thirty centimeters thick, and it took several blasts to get through each segment. After several minutes, it appeared to be cut clean through.

"Lemme try it." Ari approached the wall and gave it a firm kick. Then another.

The interior piece of the arch dropped backward with a thud and a reverberating clang.

Kira smiled. "Nice work."

Ari swapped his rifle for his handgun and passed through the archway, followed closely by Kira and the other two members of the team.

"We're coming up on the holding area," Kira said using the internal comms. "I didn't go through it before, but I saw it on some monitors. Keep your cool."

"We've got this," Ari replied.

They had advanced another five meters down the corridor when an inhuman shriek echoed down the hall.

"What was that?!" Ari halted.

Kira grimaced. "If I had to guess, one of the Robus." She held her handgun at the ready. "Keep moving forward."

The enhanced audio receptors in Kira's armor detected approaching footsteps—what sounded more like bare feet than boots. Her HUD confirmed the approaching forms a second later. They were moving far more quickly than a person should be able to. Two of their heat signatures flickering, like they were at the edge of a spatial distortion.

"Is anyone else's HUD glitching?" Ari asked.

"That's not a glitch… Run!" Kira about-faced and sprinted toward the exit.

Proximity alerts flashed across her HUD. Before she could react, something swatted her legs out from under her.

She stumbled to the side, smacking the wall and then falling to her back.

On top of her was a person-sized creature with luminescent orange eyes. Its skin had a metallic sheen to it, muscular and scaly. The creature's lips were contorted into a snarl, revealing that the inside of its mouth was covered in the same metallic coating, its fangs shaped to tear flesh from bone. The creature's arm was poised to swipe its fifteen-centimeter-long silvery claws across Kira's neck.

Kira tried to raise her weapon, but her arm was pinned under the creature's other arm.

A sonic blast rippled through the air.

The Robus recoiled in pain and retreated down the hall. As it ran, it suddenly disappeared from view before reappearing a meter from where it had been a moment earlier.

What the…? Kira looked around and saw more than two dozen people, robed in medical gowns, running down the corridor. Their skin had a metallic sheen to it, but they didn't have claws or fangs. Though all of their eyes glowed with bioluminescence, indicating Gifted abilities, none were orange. Her team was busy subduing them with sonic blasts. Kira leaped to her feet and joined in.

"You okay, Captain?" Kyle asked when the final opponent fell.

"Yeah. Thanks to whoever got that thing off me."

"You're welcome," Ari replied.

Twenty-six unconscious hybrid creatures lay in the hall. They began transforming back into their normal forms.

"There were two that weren't like the others," Nia commented.

"I think those must have been the Robus," Kira surmised. "I guess the procedure didn't take like it was supposed to."

"Did you see how they were moving?" Kyle shook his head with wonder.

"Was it 'stopping time'—that thing TSS Agents can supposedly do?" Nia wondered.

Kira frowned. "That's a really rare skill, as I understand. And a misnomer—they just create a spatial distortion around themselves, like initiating a mini-spatial jump."

"Oh, 'just'." Ari snorted.

"Regardless, we should proceed as if the Robus have that ability. We'll need to be extra careful now that they likely know they're cornered."

"You don't say?" Kyle tightened his grip on his weapon.

"How many total captives did you say there are?" Ari asked.

Kira shook her head. "Jared said one hundred, but I wasn't able to confirm. More than are in this hallway, for sure, from what I saw on the monitors. And that's not counting however many were taken from town last night."

"The four of us can't subdue that many if they're all this aggressive," Kyle stated the obvious.

"We should fall back and come in with a bigger team and more concussion grenades," Kira suggested.

"Hey, she's coming around!" Nia approached a woman lying near her. She kept her distance and had her weapon ready to fire. "Do you know who you are?"

The young woman startled awake. "Yes, I'm... I'm Emmie." She sat up. "Where am I?"

Kira stepped toward her. "You're in an MTech lab. Do you remember anything?"

"I've been in a cell, I think." Emmie grasped her head. "Where's Melissa? She was..."

"I don't know—" Kira cut off when she noticed the other people rousing.

Questioning murmurs filled the hall.

"It looks like they're themselves," she told her team using the internal comms. "Let's start the evac while they're manageable."

Keeping their guns ready just in case anyone started to revert, Kira's team shepherded the captives toward the exit.

"We're coming out with twenty-six right now," Kira messaged operational command and the soldiers waiting in the lobby. "We'll need concussion grenades and backup to continue the search."

Kira's group was in the final stretch of hallway leading to the lobby when she saw Colonel Kaen, Leon, and a dozen soldiers approaching.

"Leon! What are you doing in here?" Kira asked on a private channel.

"Kaen thought I should come along as a guide to help access the computer network for evidence, now that things have settled down," he replied.

"It isn't safe yet."

"If this armor is good enough to protect you, then it is for me, too."

Kira looked down at herself and realized that a new set of claw marks had been raked across her chest. *That settles it—this set is officially 'broken in'.* "But I have weapons," she countered his statement.

"And I have you."

Good point. She sighed. "Okay, just stay vigilant."

While they had been talking, two of the soldiers had begun directing the prisoners toward the exit while the others prepared to press forward toward D Wing.

"Sir, I suggest you and Leon hang back while we clear the path," Kira suggested.

Kaen nodded and allowed Kira's team to lead the way back.

The support soldiers handed two concussion grenades to her and to each member of her team. She stashed hers in a pouch at her waist.

They broke into a jog and kept the pace until they reached the point in the D Wing hall where they'd first encountered resistance. Her HUD indicated that no one was lurking around the first bend.

After the turn, the corridor opened into the observation room. An open doorway on the left wall presumably led to the holding area.

"Should be through here," Kira directed.

"And back there?" Kaen asked.

"That's a lab room—one egress point. I suspect Monica and her accomplice, Jared, are holed up in there."

Kaen nodded. "They're not going anywhere right now. I'll keep watch with a couple of soldiers while you take care of the captives. Then we can deal with them."

"Yes, sir." Kira continued toward the holding corridor.

The open doorway provided a peek of the cells. The first two cells Kira could see were empty. She stepped through the opening and passed by a three-meter segment of storage cabinets to either side, and then the passageway split in two directions. Cells lined both sides of the hall, and the doors to those on the left were open. At the end of that section, two Robus were facing off against a huddle of several dozen people together.

"Some help?!" one of the people shouted when he saw Kira.

Without hesitation, Kira fired sonic blasts with her handgun at the two Robus. It took four blasts to take them down.

A middle-aged man with dark hair at the front of the group cautiously stood up. "They couldn't be reasoned with."

"Are you injured?" Kira asked, stepping forward.

"Nothing that won't heal," he replied.

"Let's lock up the Robus until we figure out how to get them to change back," Kira said to Ari and Kyle when they came up behind her.

The two soldiers secured the creatures in cuffs and anchored them inside cells on opposite sides of the hall.

Kira spotted the door controls and sealed them inside, just in case they were able to break free.

"What happened to the others?" a woman asked.

"They're outside with our people. They attacked us while transformed, but they seemed fine once back in their standard forms," Kira replied.

"Probably thought you were one of the mercs," the first man said. "They opened all the cells at once. We were all agitated, but the others were different—like animals. Vicious killers. We all ran for the exit when the cell doors opened, but then the Robus, as you call them, came charging back, and we ended up trapped here."

"We'll get you to safety now," Kira assured him. "More of

our people are in the next room. They'll get you out."

"Thank you." He bowed his head. "I don't even know how long I've been here… or where 'here' is."

"This is the planet Valta," she told him. "We're with the Tararian Guard."

He looked surprised. "The Empire is involved?"

"Well, the Guard. The whole point is sorta that it's not official," Kira corrected.

The man nodded. "Whoever you are or whatever reason you're here, thank you. We owe you our lives."

Murmurs of thanks passed through the crowd.

She smiled. "It's what we do. But if you'll excuse us, I need to find the others. They took some locals last night."

"Other section of the hall," the man said with a nod down the corridor. "I saw them brought in."

Kira jogged toward where he'd indicated while the prisoners filed out into the outer administrative area. The first few dozen cells were empty, but then she found smiling, relieved faces pressed against the plexiglass walls. They were speaking, but no sound escaped; the comms must have been muted.

She checked down the length of cells to make sure everyone was okay, and to make sure that everyone had seen that help had arrived. Her heart skipped a beat when she reached a cell containing her father, and then another holding her mother.

Kira tore off her helmet, and her parents pressed their hands against the plexiglass. She held one of her hands out to each while looking around for a master door release, but none was to be found. She held up her index finger and then ran back to the white room.

"I found the others!" she announced. "Where're the door

controls?"

"This might be the right time to track Monica down," Kaen suggested.

"Yes, we're well overdue for an honest chat." Kira turned to Leon. "Will you go wait with the remaining prisoners in there to the right? My parents are among them. They'll recognize you—without the helmet, of course. We should have the door open in just a few minutes."

Leon slid off his helmet. "Got it." He jogged into the holding corridor.

Kira glared at the lab door the soldiers had been guarding. "Now for Monica."

CHAPTER 20

KIRA STORMED TOWARD the lab door. "If Monica thinks she can get away with hiding in here, she better reevaluate." The control panel next to the door was nonresponsive. *This isn't a room we can shoot our way into without risking too much damage. We need to examine that tech.*

"Kyle, a little help with an override?" Kira requested.

"I'm on it," her teammate replied, jogging over.

Before he had a chance to interface with the control panel, the door suddenly slid open. Kira instinctually took a step back, drawing her weapon.

Monica stood in the doorway, her hands raised in defeat. She still wore her white lab coat and seemed unfazed by having multiple weapons pointed toward her. "You have me."

"Yeah, you're foking right we do—" Kira began.

"No need to berate someone who willingly turned themself in," Kaen interjected. He approached the room. "You're Monica Waylon, the director of this facility?"

"I am," Monica acknowledged. "My assistant and I became

trapped in this lab when our medical patients broke free. They were in some kind of frenzy."

"Your 'patients'?!" Kira laughed. "We have all the evidence we need against you. You can drop the benevolent doctor act. *You* were what caused these poor people to turn vicious."

Monica's eyes narrowed the slightest measure, focusing on Colonel Kaen. "You must believe that I did what I thought was right, to help advance our species."

Kaen grunted. "I don't think so. We value the independence of people and the chance for them to choose what happens to their own bodies. Forcing genetic modification is never justified."

"And if I told you they consented?" Monica asked.

"Wouldn't believe it," Kira spat. "You're finished."

The director stepped forward through the lab's doorway with a very reluctant-looking Jared following behind. Guard soldiers kept handguns trained on the two scientists.

Monica composed her face with a prim smile. "Then I suppose you should just take me away. I have nothing more to say to you."

Jared moved aside under the watchful eye of a soldier.

"Oh, no! You're not getting off that easily," Kira said, rounding on Monica. "You've been keeping people captive in a secret underground lab and think you can just get away with, 'Oh, guess everyone knows what's going on now, sorry'? No. You're going to explain who you're working for and what you meant to get out of this—"

Colonel Kaen held up his hand to stop Kira from continuing.

Monica shook her head. "Oh, Kira, it's really too bad you didn't want to learn more about yourself when you had the chance. Your passion could have been directed into something more meaningful."

"What I'm doing here is plenty meaningful. We just helped free more than a hundred people who would have been abused until you lost interest and discarded them." Kira scoffed. "For someone who seems to think of herself as a higher being, you sure know how to act like the lowest of the low."

"Think what you will. There are stronger powers at play here than just me. Detaining me now won't alter the work that's been done."

"Then we'll find all your other labs, and whoever you're working with, and stop them, too," Kira told her.

The colonel turned toward Kira while the soldiers stayed alert with their weapons trained on the scientist.

Kira looked him in the eyes. "Let me force her, sir. 'Any means'. This mission isn't over."

"Do your worst, Captain," the colonel replied, then directed the two soldiers, "Shackle her."

"Your conviction is to be admired," Monica said as the soldiers cuffed her hands in front and shackled her legs. "You are certainly welcome to try Reading me, though you won't be successful."

Challenge accepted. Kira approached her. "I have a way of getting things done."

"Perhaps you will. I should tell you, though…" Monica reached out toward Kira as though to cup her bound hand around her ear to whisper a secret.

Kira quickly stepped back. "Yeah, gonna keep my distance, thanks."

Monica smiled. "Never mind, then. Maybe you're better off not knowing."

"Uh, Captain…" Nia cut in. "The cell doors?"

"Right!" Kira's original task came back to her. "Log into the computer system, Monica. I could force you, but we both know it will end the same way."

Monica rolled her eyes. "You really think I'll just hand over the keys that easily?"

The three members of Kira's team advanced on the scientist.

Kira smirked. "I'm thinking you might."

Monica looked the three soldiers up and down like she couldn't be bothered with them, but she sighed. "No need to be that way about it." She shuffled toward the computer console in the center of the room.

The three soldiers stayed on her heels with Kira close behind. They watched over Monica's shoulder while she logged into the system then immediately prodded her away from the computer before she could try anything nefarious.

"That wasn't so hard, was it?" Kira asked.

"Oh, you have no idea," the other woman replied. She looked to Colonel Kaen. "You have access to my systems. Are we done here?"

Kaen met her gaze and nodded. "We'll finish the interrogation at Orion Station. I'll escort her out." The colonel motioned for the soldiers who weren't on Kira's team to take charge of the prisoner.

"We need to secure him, as well." One soldier nodded toward Jared, who'd continued to stand still while the assigned guard stood menacingly over him.

"Yes, we'll release the remaining prisoners and move out," Kaen agreed. "Kira, why don't you and Leon begin going through the computer system and pull out the relevant information?"

"Yes, sir, we're on it," Kira acknowledged. She scanned over the panel and located the controls for the cell doors. A master switch was divided into west and east sections. She activated the unlock for only the east, remembering the two Robus they had put in the cells in the western cellblock.

"Should be open now," she announced. "And you should check on the other two captives we subdued earlier to see if they've shifted back."

"Robus?" Kaen prompted.

Kira nodded. "The nanotech seems to make some sort of overlay on them, filtering through their skin to and merging to augment certain features. I've never seen anything like it."

"I look forward to reviewing the footage from your combat recorder," Kaen said.

"Definitely got up close and personal."

The colonel nodded slowly. "I hope whatever was done to them can be reversed."

Monica scoffed in response.

"Maybe Leon can take a look at the research and see what he can figure out," Kira suggested.

"Excellent," Kaen agreed.

Voices carried from the holding area while the townspeople began to file out. Kira spotted her parents in the middle of the crowd with Leon. They smiled at her and she ran to them.

"Are you okay?!" she exclaimed. "I'm sorry, I didn't know they—"

"Don't apologize, sweetheart," her mother soothed.

Her father nodded. "We made it out just fine, thanks to you and your team."

Anger welled in Kira's chest. "You never should have been placed in that position. MTech—"

"You stopped them," Harold said. "We're only free now because of you."

Their dismissal didn't change the fact that her parents had been at the mercy of a deranged psychopath. "Did they do anything to you?" she asked.

"They injected us with something, but there haven't been signs of a change," Ruth replied, surprisingly calm. "We overheard one of the scientists say something about an error in the coding and that we were useless until it left our systems."

"Still feel like myself!" Harold patted his chest.

"We'll need to verify that with the experiment logs and testing, but that fits with what I overheard. I'm sure it will be fine," Kira assured them, hoping it was true. She looked at the activity around the room. "I'd see you out, but there's still a lot to do around here."

"It's so different seeing you like this," her father murmured.

"All I could think about while I was in that cell was that I never should have tried to change you," her mother said, tears forming in her eyes. "You've been telling us all this time how you joined the Guard to help people, but I never wanted to admit that there were bad people out there in the universe."

The words caught Kira by surprise. "I always wanted to *prevent* something like this from happening on Valta."

"You've stopped any more harm from being done," her father said. He paused, seeming to fight back his own tears. "If your gifts can help make other worlds safer, then we can be very proud parents."

The statement was what Kira had sought to hear for most of her adult life—to be accepted for who she was and everything she could contribute. It would take time to rebuild a relationship with her parents based on that newfound understanding, but this was a start. "Thanks, Dad."

He gathered himself. "We should leave you to it."

Kira's Guard duties likely wouldn't take her back to Valta anytime soon. This was the best chance she'd get to solidify the reconnection with her parents. *I don't want to spend another decade regretting all of the things I should have said.*

She took a step closer to them. "Hey, I'll be busy for a while, but maybe we could get a late lunch or dinner?"

"We look forward to it." Her mother reached up to brush the hair from Kira's forehead.

Her father smiled. "We're so proud of you, Kira."

The words filled her with a warm glow. "See you soon."

Kira's parents took each other's hands and followed the last of the townspeople out the exit.

She turned back toward the workstations. "Leon, can you help with the data extraction?"

"Sure. I'll get started." He gave her a knowing smile and nodded. There was no way he could have overheard the details, but he had no doubt picked up on the gist of the conversation with her parents; more than anyone, he knew how much that validation meant to Kira.

Four soldiers entered the holding area to retrieve the Robus. Kira wasn't sure four would be remotely sufficient if the creatures were still in a mindless rage, but she figured they'd call for backup if it looked like it was going to be a problem.

Two minutes later, the four soldiers returned escorting a ragged-looking woman and a muscular man.

The woman's face dropped when she caught sight of Kira. "I'm so sorry! I didn't know what I was doing."

"I'm fine," Kira told her. "This armor is built to take a beating."

"Even still—" The woman cut off when she saw Monica. "You! You bitch!" She tried to charge the scientist, but the soldiers stopped her.

"Get her out of here!" Kira instructed when she noticed the woman's eyes taking on an orange cast.

The guards hurriedly complied.

Monica watched her go with a surprisingly smug expression.

"She knew you." Kira evaluated Monica. "Did you do something extra-special to piss her off, beyond just being your charming mad-scientist self?"

"Poor Tim got too attached to her before his accident. Melissa didn't take the news of his passing well."

Kira barely resisted attacking Monica herself. She took a deep breath while she waited for the guards escorting the Robus to get a sufficient head start.

The colonel watched his soldiers go. "Captain, you and Leon keep working on the computer. I'll need to borrow your team to secure this prisoner."

"With pleasure," Ari said while he, Kyle, and Nia positioned to flank Monica.

"Sir, we should keep her under heavier guard than that," Kira objected. "Her abilities—"

Kaen hesitated, but his expression suddenly relaxed. "We'll be fine, Captain. Proceed with the system investigation."

"Yes, sir," she acknowledged.

The remaining soldier went ahead with Jared, and then Kira's team followed Monica while Kaen brought up the rear.

Once they were out of sight, Kira allowed herself a moment to relax. "How can anyone be so cold?"

"It's like she's lost track of what it means to have a free life," Leon replied from the computer monitor. "She was a bit detached when I interacted with her before, but I never saw anything like this."

"At least she can't hurt anyone else." Kira came around the

middle of the computer station so she could see what Leon was working on. "Is everything unlocked?"

"Yeah, I'm working my way through it now. I found a summary report that indicates there were only two semi-successful Robus conversions from the Stage Two trials, so that explains Melissa and the man... didn't catch his name."

"And then Stage Three was converting a non-telekinetic person into a hybrid. But it sounds like they didn't get it quite right."

"Thank the stars. I wouldn't want to think about what would happen if a strain of nanites like that got out."

"No kidding." Kira slipped off the gloves of her powered armor so she could type more freely. "I'll help you look around. We need all the information we can get to see if we can reverse whatever was done to these people."

— — —

Joris stared at the signed digital document in front of him. With its submission, the Elusian Alliance was officially part of the Taran Empire. No longer were the Elusians and Mysarans just two governments fighting over a third world in their small system, but, rather, the Elvar Trinary now had direct ties to something much greater. Whether his Mysaran neighbors would willingly embrace that reality was yet to be seen.

Ellen had remained across the desk from Joris while he made the final arrangements for the signing. Her face was drawn and her arms were crossed.

"Do you think this was the right call?" Joris asked.

"I'm probably not the best person to be asking, considering that I was ready to kill in order to keep anyone in this system from rejoining the Empire."

"That's precisely why I want to know what you think."

She considered the statement. "Yes, I do believe this was for the best. The mentality that we should remain separate is an old way of thinking that won't move us forward. Unity is what's best."

Achieving that unity would be a long road, Joris knew, but his people might not have had a future if he'd continued to delay a decision. With Chancellor Hale on alert, the entire Mysaran fleet could be directed toward Elusia at any moment. It would only take several well-placed shots to level the cities on his world, should they choose to take such aggressive action.

"I hope the Mysarans see reason," he murmured.

"They'd be foolish to move against an Empire world. Even if the Empire didn't directly retaliate, they could still make life difficult and unpleasant. These three worlds need each other— Mysar on its own isn't sustainable."

"It's funny how interdependent current worlds have become. To think how our ancestors lived so long on one planet..."

"Advancement causes us to rethink how we interact with the rest of the universe," Ellen pointed out.

"True." Joris took a deep breath. "I'm anxious for the Mysarans' response. The Empire's warning to halt their ship should have been received by now."

"Yes. I wonder—"

The desktop lit up with notice of an incoming call.

"And there she is!" Joris tapped his desk to accept the video call from the Mysaran Chancellor. "Madam Chancellor, I trust you have received news of our unification with the Empire?"

The woman glared at him through the screen. "Yes, we did indeed. I'm surprised you'd let them sway you so easily."

"This was a long time coming. But they didn't force our

hand—you did. I won't let my people live in fear of your military threats. You'd be foolish to take any action against us now."

"And you think that by signing an agreement we want nothing to do with, you will improve our relations? Bah!" She threw up her hands. "You've just signed an extension of your slow decline."

Joris kept his tone calm and measured. "I know the resources of your world just as well as you know mine. We are better off together than we are apart. The Empire is no longer how they were before the Priesthood's fall—censoring information and controlling people's lives. We have an opportunity to be a part of the Empire's rebirth. Our people can seek education and employment on worlds throughout the galaxy, and beyond. We can benefit from the shared technology. To remain isolationist is to condemn our people to a narrow life of tedium when a whole universe of possibilities exists out there for the taking. Why are you so bent on keeping us here by ourselves?"

The chancellor's face twisted. "I... I—" she sputtered, unable to complete the words.

"Chancellor, are you all right?" Joris asked.

Ellen's brow furrowed with concern across the desk.

"There's this compulsion," the chancellor said at last. "I've had it for as long as I can remember. Everyone in our government does. It's just the way we are. We must stay alone."

"That defies logic. You must have a reason *why*," Joris pressed.

"I understand that on a rational level, but something else within me is compelled to keep us alone." The chancellor's pale green eyes were wild, as though she were accessing some part of herself that she hadn't recognized before.

"I don't understand." Joris watched her labored movements. *Something is going on here... She's always seen reason, even when she doesn't agree. A 'compulsion' isn't the reasoning of a sane person.*

Chancellor Hale's face suddenly transformed to a neutral expression. "President Joris, you must forgive my statements earlier. I was distressed over this discovery that you had moved ahead with the reunification before we could come to an accord. I must take time to process this development. You need have no immediate fears of Mysaran military action." The call ended.

Joris' mouth dropped opened. "What the fok just happened?"

Ellen shook her head side to side. "I have no idea, sir. It was almost like she was... possessed."

"That was my thought, too. But... by what?"

"I don't know, sir," Ellen murmured. "If she is under the influence of someone, or something, it *would* connect with the information leaks."

"Fok!" Joris groaned. "There's no way to predict what she might do. Who could we even tell about this?"

"What about your contact at the Guard?" Ellen suggested. "They must have the resources to investigate a matter like this covertly and figure out what to do."

"Yes, I suspect that's our best option."

Ellen nodded. "In the meantime, we should prepare a statement informing our people of the reunification. There'll be some dissent, I'm sure, but what you said to Chancellor Hale right now makes a very compelling argument: the universe is our people's if they want it, and if not, Elusia will always be a home."

"Yes, let's make a statement. I'll ask the Guard to look into

Mysar's government as soon as the situation with Valta is resolved."

Ellen leaned forward in her chair. "I was thinking for the opening line, 'You now have the means to make your own future'."

Joris smiled. "I like it."

CHAPTER 21

KAEN FOLLOWED THE other soldiers at a distance, watching Monica's movements. She glanced back at him on occasion, as if waiting for him to say something else.

What would I possibly have to say to her outside of an interrogation room? He kept his gaze ahead, trying to ignore her.

After a minute, and several more glances, Monica finally let out a loud sigh. "Fine, then *I'll* make the move." Her cuffs seemed to fall to the ground of their own accord.

She moved faster than Kaen could track, knocking Kyle's and Ari's heads together, throwing Nia to the ground, and tackling the other soldier leading Jared. Unfortunately for Jared, he was pinned under the soldier's armor when he fell.

In the blink of an eye, Monica grabbed spare stasis cuffs from the soldiers' waistbands and tethered the Guard soldiers to the floor, then ripped out the comm systems from their armor.

Kaen watched the attack happening before his eyes, frozen

in place.

Does she have me under some sort of telepathic influence? It was possible—Kira had warned him about Monica's abilities, though Kaen hadn't expected to experience the skills firsthand. All he knew was that he was trapped inside his own body, and it made him furious.

Monica finished securing the soldiers and stood up. She used her thumb and forefinger to remove contacts from her eyes, revealing glowing gray irises.

"A little help?" Jared called, unsuccessfully trying to pry the heavy, unconscious soldier off him.

"No, this must look convincing. Stay quiet." She turned to Kaen. "Don't go anywhere." She slammed his head against the wall.

— — —

"Ooo, this is good!" Kira dragged another collection of lab reports into a 'best of' directory she was compiling. "And by 'good', I mean these people are foking monsters."

"Yeah, I'm getting the impression that the higher-ups at MTech are an unsavory lot," Leon agreed. "I feel sick that I was working for them."

"You didn't know. And what *you* were working on wasn't this."

"Yeah, but still…" He shook his head. "I have some making up to do."

"I think there's a lot of that to go around." She gave him a supportive smile.

"Kira Elsar! I still have that secret to tell you."

Kira's heart leaped when she saw Monica in the doorway, irises glowing. "The f—"

Monica waved her hand, and Kira careened across the room before she could react. She slammed into the side wall, propelled by an unseen force. Her skin tingled with electrical energy. The doctor rushed up to where Kira was pinned, looming over her.

Even with Kira in powered armor, the other woman's telekinetic strength gave her the advantage. Worse, without her gloves, Kira's hands were useless for punching or grabbing. Desperate, Kira tried to elbow Monica away from her and get in a jab with her knee, but Monica's reactions were always one step ahead.

"Stay... still!" Monica's movements were a blur as Kira struggled to get free.

A cool prick registered on Kira's wrist, and she twisted her arm away.

"You'll make quite the prize," Monica whispered. Then louder, "I'll make you mine."

"The fok you will!" Leon appeared behind Monica and looped his arm around her neck.

The doctor telekinetically flung Leon off of her, his inexperience in the powered armor no match for her skills.

Kira, however, seized the opportunity. She lunged forward and locked the doctor in a chokehold with her powered armor. Monica sputtered and gasped, ripping at Kira with half-formed telekinetic counterattacks. Kira wasn't about to let go, pushing through each of the armor's automated stops, squeezing tighter. Suddenly, Monica's head jerked at an unnatural angle with a sickening pop.

Startled, Kira released her grasp, and the doctor's body dropped to the floor, head lolling to the side with mouth agape in shocked horror. Kira stumbled backward, chest heaving. Her hands were shaking uncontrollably.

"It's okay. It's over," Leon whispered to her, running over. He placed a reassuring arm around her shoulders.

"Bitch didn't know when to give up."

Leon averted his gaze from the corpse. "She won't be coming back from this one."

"Yeah, I probably shouldn't have done that." Kira swallowed. "I couldn't let her get away with what she's done..."

"She had it coming," Leon agreed. He looked her over with concern. "Are you okay, Kira? It looked like she was messing with some sort of syringe."

Kira touched the spot on her wrist where she'd felt the cool prick. It was a bit tender, but she felt fine. "She might not have been able to dose me, with all the tumbling around. I don't feel any different."

"Given what went on here—"

"I'll go in for a full medical screening as soon as we're back at Guard headquarters. Our doctors are the best—the whole science support team, actually."

He still looked worried but nodded.

"What the...?" Kaen appeared in the doorway, a welt on his forehead.

"Colonel!" Kira exclaimed. "What happened? Monica—"

"She overpowered us, knocked everyone out," the colonel explained. "The others are rousing now. I came back as quickly as I could. She said she was coming for you."

"Yeah, she tried to stick me with a syringe."

"Successfully?"

"I'm not sure," Kira admitted. "Didn't go so well for her in the end."

Kaen grunted. "So much for being able to interrogate her."

"Sorry, Colonel. That thought wasn't front and center while she was trying to kill me."

"Based on what I've found so far, Jared will be able to offer valuable insights," Leon offered. "Not sure if he was connected to the boss like Monica, but in terms of the tech, he knows his stuff."

"And honestly," Kira added, "she was never going to talk. A telepath like her would be impervious to any interrogation technique we could throw at her."

"Then perhaps it's for the best." Kaen tore his gaze away from the body. "Finish the data transfer and meet us outside. And make sure to get yourself cleared by Medical." He departed without another word.

"Was he angry?" Kira asked Leon when her superior officer was gone. "I can't tell if he was angry."

"I think he was embarrassed that she escaped."

Kira took a deep breath. "I'm not happy about that, either—or anything that's gone on here."

He took her hand. "You're *sure* you're okay?"

"We're alive—can't complain."

Leon smiled back at her. "All right. But you have to go to Medical as soon as we're finished."

"No more worrying." Kira returned her attention to the computer console. "Let's finish transferring this data. I can't wait to get out of here."

CHAPTER 22

THE SUN WAS well above the horizon by the time Kira and Leon emerged from the MTech facility.

Monica's body had been removed while they worked, and Nia had had the foresight to bring them some protein bars to munch on when she returned to the lab to help out. The three of them had transferred all the information they could find related to the genetic experimentation to external drives, prepping the data for the exhaustive analysis process. Nia had gone ahead with the drives while Leon helped Kira do one final sweep of the lab. With everything now shut down and secure, they could finally begin processing the night's events.

Kira shed her powered armor as soon as she was outside, seeing that no one else was in their combat gear. "I'd like to distance myself from what happened this morning as much as possible," she said while staring at the new claw marks on the chest-plate.

"Same." Leon stepped out from his own armor. "I don't know how you do it."

"Today was the exception, not the rule," Kira replied. "Normally it's 'covert' ops, not 'blow the front door and break people's necks' ops."

"An important distinction."

"We like to think so."

He eyed her. "So, what now?"

Kira's stomach growled; that protein bar hadn't held her for long. "In order of personal preference? Proper breakfast, shower, and decompressing time." *Let's see if he takes that hint.*

"We *were* about to have an important discussion before we were interrupted last night," he replied, picking up on her meaning.

"One I look forward to finishing." She flashed a winning smile. "I also promised my parents lunch or dinner together today—no need to sit in on that, unless you want to."

"Of course, I'd love to come along."

And he likes my parents. Stars, now I'm suspicious that he was engineered himself. She beamed. "All right, it's a date."

Kira excused herself from Leon so she could check in with her team. Ari, Nia, and Kyle were gathered under a temporary overhang that had been erected near the landing craft.

"That was intense," Kyle said when he saw Kira approaching.

"Yeah, two firefights in a week is a bit much," she agreed. "You all okay? I know Monica did a number on you earlier."

Ari shook his head. "That 'stopping time' trick is something else. I was blacked out before I even saw her move."

"Nia filled us in on what happened while we were out," Kyle added. "Sounds like things got a little up close and personal for you."

"I showed Monica what was what." Kira grimaced.

Nia placed her hand on Kira's shoulder. "Better this way—

can't trust someone like that."

"I know." Kira rubbed her eyes with the heels of her hands. "And once we know more about what was done to those poor people…"

Kyle nodded. "I talked to some of them while we were debriefing. They were from all over. MTech must have been at it for months."

"We need to find out if there are any other places like this. I hate to think there's anyone else being held against their will," Kira said.

"You're in luck." Ari smiled. "Delivering justice for the disenfranchised happens to be the Guard's specialty."

She grinned back at him, the weight on her lifting. "I wouldn't have it any other way."

"I gave the data drives to Major Sandren," Nia said in the ensuing pause. "The colonel seemed a little distracted."

"Thanks. That knock on his head was probably harder than he wants to admit," Kira replied.

"We do take our pride very personally," Ari pointed out.

"Seeing a big lug like you get knocked over had to have made him feel a little better," Kira needled.

Ari grunted. "Monica just caught me by surprise."

"Uh huh…" Kira walked away. She knew how much he hated being left hanging.

Leon was just coming over the crest of the hill, and she jogged up to him. As she neared, she saw he was frowning.

"What's wrong?" she asked.

"I just saw them affixing a giant 'Condemned' sign to the lab."

"Oh." She crossed her arms. "I imagine the facility will be under investigation for some time. I'm sorry things had to go down this way."

"Well, I guess I really am out of a job," he muttered.

"This one, maybe," Kaen said, coming up behind them.

"Sir." Kira nodded to him.

"You showed great initiative on this mission," Kaen continued. "We could use a person like you in the Guard."

Leon's violet eyes widened with surprise. "Are you... offering me a position?"

"I am, indeed. What do you say?" The colonel looked around. "This is a beautiful planet, I'll give you that, but there aren't a lot of other opportunities here for someone with your training."

"I'm not much of a soldier, sir. After today, I'm certain I don't have the stomach for it."

"Oh, no, no. The position I had in mind was as civilian consultant with our science division. The nanotech research they were doing here was woefully misguided, but elements of it would go a long way toward helping us get the most out of our soldiers. You could continue your research with the backing of the Taran Empire's resources."

"I—I don't know what to say," Leon stammered.

" 'Yes' would be a good answer." Kaen smiled.

Leon glanced at Kira. "I'll let you know soon."

Kaen's gaze flitted between Kira and Leon. "I look forward to your acceptance." He left them to their discussion.

Kira kicked her toe into the dirt, nervous for what his answer might be. After the last few days together, the idea of parting ways again was difficult to stomach. Having both the Guard *and* Leon had always seemed unattainable, but it now seemed feasible for the first time.

"Whaddya think?" Leon asked her.

"It's your decision," she said. *I don't know if I deserve a second chance to win back his trust, but right now I want nothing more.*

"The Guard was always your thing. I don't want to cramp your style."

"You joining the Guard as a researcher doesn't change anything."

He took her hand. "What if I want it to? I think the last few days have shown we still make a pretty good team."

A slow smile spread across Kira's face. "Not gonna lie—the prospect of going back to base without you kinda sucked."

"I was hoping you'd say that."

Her heart leaped. "You sure you want to give this another go?"

"If you're good with me accepting the colonel's offer."

"Stars, yes!" She threw her arms around his neck and whispered in his ear, "I don't want to let you go again, either."

Over Leon's shoulder, across the lawn, she saw Ari tap Kyle on the shoulder and point to Kira. Nia's and Kyle's mouths dropped open, and Ari chuckled. In true form, Ari grabbed his helmet and activated the combat recorder.

Kira shook her head with exasperation, then locked Leon in a passionate kiss. *May as well give them something filmworthy.*

— — —

Representatives from the Elusian media were waiting patiently in the lobby of the capitol building for President Joris to take the podium. He checked himself over, and Ellen gave a nod of approval. Joris nodded back and stepped into place.

Amidst the reporters were citizens from all walks of life, anxious to hear the urgent statement he'd make this afternoon.

Joris took a deep breath and began. "You now have the

means to make your own future. When our ancestors set out generations ago to settle this system, it was to start a new life that would enable them to achieve their dreams of freedom and prosperity. But that hasn't always been the case. We have been at odds with our neighbors and competing for what no one should rightfully control.

"There is another way. The Taran Empire stands as a beacon of unity and empowerment. They do not seek to control or dictate, but rather to share and offer mutual benefit. Some of us have lived in fear that joining with the Empire would consume the heart of our culture. That isn't the case. What they offer is for us to make that culture all it can be, and to learn and grow as we continue to refine our identity and shape the future we want for coming generations.

"We have argued amongst ourselves about what the best way forward is, but I couldn't allow civil conflicts to continue escalating. I made the decision that, as your elected leader, I feel is most representative of our people's wishes, and that will give us the best chance to achieve the future vision we share.

"That act was to officially reintegrate Elusia into the Taran Empire."

The crowd erupted in a cacophony of questions, cheers, and a few shouts of protest.

Joris held up his hands to quiet them. "I know this won't please everyone, and while I would have preferred for this to be handled through our democratic process, we were short on time. Political tensions are running high, and Valta continues to be a point of contention between the Elusian Alliance and Mysaran Coalition. I feared that any delays in signing this agreement may have resulted in hardships for our people. This should be a time of joy for what's to come, not of worry that danger is lurking around the corner.

"As a full member planet of the Taran Empire, we now have all the protections of their military. We have their science, their schools, and their transportation network. The limitless possibilities of the universe are now within reach," he smiled, "though that might be a bit too poetic. Through it all, we will still be Elusia. We come from Taran heritage, but we are Elusians now, and will remain Elusians in the Empire. Let us celebrate!"

Joris took a step back from the podium as the crowd cheered once more—this time drowning out any 'boos' that may have been uttered. He soaked in their enthusiasm, thankful that his announcement seemed to have been taken as a positive move.

He leaned in toward the microphone again. "I'm sure you have many questions about the timeline for integration and the specifics of what expanded services will now be available. My office will be preparing a detailed statement in the coming days. For the time being, enjoy the knowledge that good things are ahead. Thank you!"

While the reporters in front shouted questions, Joris made a quick retreat with Ellen.

"That was wonderfully delivered," Ellen told him. "I was watching their faces, and I think the consensus is positive."

"We'll see how the analysts pick it apart."

"Given the situation with Mysar, this remains the right call," Ellen assured him.

"I hope others come to see it that way, too." Joris let out a long breath. "Now that that's over, I must attend to some other business."

"Yes, sir, of course." Ellen shifted on her feet.

"Was there something else?" he prompted.

She crossed her arms and looked down. "I confessed a

planned treasonous act to you earlier. What will become of me?"

"You said you no longer have plans to kill me. Does that remain the case?"

"Knowing what I know now, I would protect your life by giving my own," she replied.

"Then what could have been never was, and so shall never be."

Her face screwed up for a moment while processing the words, then smiled. "Need anything else today?"

"No, take the evening for yourself. I suspect we'll be at it bright and early tomorrow. If you're up for it, I'd like you to lead the team that's compiling the statement about reintegration and its benefits."

Ellen inclined her head. "I'd be honored, sir."

"Excellent. Have a good night." He waved farewell.

Joris returned to his office for one final task before he could rest easy for the night. The conversation with the Mysaran chancellor still had him on edge.

He knew Colonel Kaen was likely still on Valta dealing with cleanup, so he sent a secure email communication for him to address once he was back at Guard Headquarters.

He kept the message concise: >>*Chancellor Hale may not be herself. Possible connection to the subversions within the Guard. Investigate immediately.*<<

Elusia may now have the Guard's protection, but they weren't out of danger yet.

— — —

Kira hopped off the medical exam bed. "So, nothing anomalous?"

"All clear," Doctor Elric replied. "Have you been feeling okay?"

"Great, aside from being unusually hungry."

"That's not surprising after the amount of activity you've had." The Guard doctor opened the door. "Rest up. Your stress indicators were higher than I'd like."

"You should know by now that's normal for me."

"Doesn't mean it *should* be that way," the doctor chastised. "Rest."

With Leon being here, I'm not sure how much sleep I'll be getting in the near future, but releasing tension I can do. She hid her smirk. "Yes, Doctor."

Kira wound her way through the station's corridors, taking a leisurely pace to her quarters. It was more of a home to her than Valta had been since she was a teenager, but she now had the most important piece from her former home here, as well— and even the relationship with her parents was on the mend. While perhaps not a perfect arrangement, things were the best they'd been in years.

She found Leon leaning against the wall outside her quarters. "How'd it go?"

"Healthy as can be. Though, I am under strict medical orders for some stress relief."

He grinned. "Say no more."

Indeed, few words were spoken over the next half hour. As she basked in the afterglow of the lovemaking, it was clear that the doctor's prescription for stress relief had been filled.

"I missed you," Kira murmured into the crook of Leon's arm.

"I missed you, too." He kissed her forehead.

Kira traced her finger down his bare, toned chest. "I don't really know how to do relationships, but I want to try."

"I'm out of practice myself. I think the fact that we've been missing each other after a decade apart indicates things will be just fine."

"Won't argue with that." She nestled closer to him.

They lay together for a while longer until Leon dozed off. Kira eventually dragged herself out of bed and wandered into the bathroom.

She cupped her hands under the cool water and leaned over the sink to splash her face. As she wiped the water away, Kira gazed into the wall mirror. Her heart skipped a beat. Gone were the hazel eyes she'd had her whole life—her irises were glowing orange.

"Well, shite."

THE STORY CONTINUES IN *CONSPIRACY*...

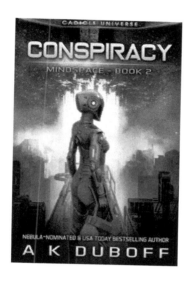

Kira's greatest opponent may be herself.

Following her exposure to experimental nanotech, Captain Kira Elsar faces an uncertain future. But uncontrollable transformations aren't her only problem.

A previously undetected alien menace, a race capable of remote telepathic control, is threatening her home system... and the Tararian Guard. With the discovery that a government official in Kira's home system has been subverted, Kira's team must get control of the situation before the Elvar Trinary descends into chaos.

ALSO BY A.K. DUBOFF

Mindspace Series
Book 1: Infiltration
Book 2: Conspiracy
Book 3: Offensive
Book 4: Endgame

Cadicle Space Opera Series
Book 1: Rumors of War (Vol. 1-3)
Book 2: Web of Truth (Vol. 4)
Book 3: Crossroads of Fate (Vol. 5)
Book 4: Path of Justice (Vol. 6)
Book 5: Scions of Change (Vol. 7)

Dark Stars Trilogy
Book 1: Crystalline Space
Book 2: A Light in the Dark
Book 3: Masters of Fate

Troubled Space
Vol. 1: Brewing Trouble
Vol. 2: Stealing Trouble
Vol. 3: Making Trouble

AUTHOR'S NOTES

Thank you for reading this first book in the Mindspace series!

There were many steps along the way for this series to become what it is today. The journey began almost two years ago, when I reached out to Michael Anderle and Craig Martelle about writing in the Age of Expansion within the Kurtherian Gambit Universe. The opportunity allowed me to quit my 'day job' so I could write full-time, and I can't express enough thanks to Michael, Craig, and the rest of the LMBPN family and JIT readers for helping me to take that initial plunge!

Working with them, this Mindspace series was originally published as the Uprise Saga. In that iteration, the Robus were Hochste, a form of Were-Vampire. For anyone familiar with Cadicle, that wouldn't fit well with the universe cannon. When I found out that I'd been able to get my rights back to this series and republish, I started thinking about how I could rework everything.

One element that the original Cadicle series didn't have was properly alien-y aliens, so I took this as an opportunity to begin weaving some truly foreign biology into the storyline. The political unrest in the Elvar Trinary was an ideal transition to the post-Priesthood era in Cadicle, so everything started to fall into place perfectly.

I wanted to be sure to draw direct connections to the original Cadicle series and planned Taran Empire sequel series. General Allen Lucian, introduced in Cadicle Volume 7, is the commanding officer over Kira's base; how he got to be in that position will be revealed in later books. I have some other crossovers and character cameos planned, but I don't want to spoil anything for what's to come in Mindspace!

I'd like to thank John, Jim, Leo, Eric, Pam, Kurt, Tracey, Troy, Charlie, Randy, Curtis, and Deborah for their tireless beta reading assistance, as well as the original JIT readers on Uprise Saga. You have so many great ideas and have such amazing eyes for language. Thank you also to Jen McDonnell for editing, and to Diane, Nick, Angel, and the rest of my incredible proofing team for adding the final polish to the book.

To my amazing husband, Nick, thank you for supporting me. Almost two years ago, he gave the go-ahead for me to quit my day job to write full-time. I am so very lucky to have him as my best friend and life partner. I'd dreamed of being an author since I was a little girl, but I never imagined I'd be able to make that dream a reality.

Thank you again for reading, and I hope you will continue reading the Mindspace series as Kira's story unfolds!

ABOUT THE AUTHOR

A.K. (Amy) DuBoff has always loved science fiction in all its forms—books, movies, shows and games. If it involves outer space, even better!

Now a full-time author, Amy can frequently be found traveling the world. When she's not writing, she enjoys wine tasting, binge-watching TV series, and playing epic strategy board games.

To learn more or connect, visit www.amyduboff.com.

Printed in Great Britain
by Amazon

41275992R00146